RENEGADE
heart

RENEGADES BOOK 1

LISSA LYNN THOMAS

For KJ who had to say goodbye before the book was finished, and who I miss dearly every single day.

Chloe

"WHY DID IT HAVE TO BE AN OUTDOOR WEDDING?" I GRUMBLE to no one in particular as I wipe sweat from my brow. My face is damp once more in a matter of seconds, and so I return to my attempts to tie the perfect little pink tulle bows to the backs of the white folding chairs assembled in the town square.

The bride, of course, is too busy being made to look perfect by her mother and her hairdresser. Apparently, it doesn't matter if the maid of honor has time to make herself presentable. I glance down at my dusty cutoff denim shorts and white tank top and wonder if Pippa—the bride—will murder me if I show up to the ceremony looking like this. I sigh as sweat trickles down my back, and then jump when I hear the low chuckle of my best friend, Raif.

"You look to be melting, Chloe Jane." Raif's deep voice skitters over my skin and I hold in a shiver.

I blow a stray strand of my heavy dark hair out of my eyes and find him standing close, his tall build shimmering in its sunshine outline. I blink to bring him into focus and grin despite my irritation at his bride to be. He looks good, even in his basketball shorts and white wife beater tank. I can tell he just rolled out of bed and ambled over to check out the square before there were people here.

"Good morning, cupcake. Yeah, I'm not built for this season. Bring me October weather and football, and I'll be a happy girl again."

His rich laugh rolls over me again, and I smile wider at him, genuinely happy to see him.

"Well, I'm pretty sure the summer will fly by," he cajoles. "You'll be back in your ten layers of clothes, hollering at us boys to follow your directions so we can win before you know it."

I sigh heavily. "Work your magic on mother nature, Raif. I can't take this heat and Pippa *forgot* to tell me last night these damn bows had to be on the back of *every* chair."

That same lock of hair falls into my eyes and before I can do more than growl at it, Raif's strong, cool fingers are on my skin. I'm pretty sure I stop breathing as his fingers work my hair out of my eyes. I feel his hand move slowly through the heavy tresses and then he's tucking the wayward strands behind my ear. When his touch tickles over the shell of my ear, I feel my pulse jump. My knees go jello-like at the same time and I clamp my bottom lip between my teeth to hold in an embarrassing, needy sound.

"There you go." He says, his voice soft, his large solid form much nearer now. I swallow down a groan and meet his bright blue-green eyes.

"Thank you," I murmur, and then straighten away from him

when the urge to lean up and press my lips to his becomes too powerful. Kissing him would be bad. He smiles his small, sweet smile down at me and brushes his knuckles over my cheekbone gently, making my stomach flop around.

"You're welcome." His voice is quiet in the little space there is between us. I swallow, trying to bring moisture into my suddenly dry mouth.

There is no air anywhere. None. He's standing too close and I can't breathe. I might pass out. That would not be helpful. What was I doing? Why am I out here wilting in the summer sun? Bows! I'm hanging bows. For his *wedding*. *Lord, Chloe, get it together.*

I hold up one of the dastardly pink things and take a shaky step backwards, away from him. "I have about a zillion more of these to hang. You should be getting ready. If you don't mind, though, you can send Vi to help me if she's got the time?" I sound strangled, but luckily, he simply holds my eyes for a beat longer and then nods, as though he's coming out of a fog.

He squares his shoulders and gives me his barely-there grin, making my heart flutter a bit harder inside my chest. "Alright, alright. I suppose you're right. I'll send Mom right out, she's been ready for ages."

I grin at him. "Thank you!" I sound way too happy.

This is what happens when you fall in love with your best friend and don't have a shot. You spend your whole life trying to act like he doesn't make your insides squirm. I watch him walk away from me and swallow down the longing that's clawing its way up my throat. I close my eyes, beating back the tears that are suddenly prickling behind them. I know better than to want more than what I have. Raif's my best friend and he loves Pippa. That's what matters.

Three hours later, the sun is even hotter, glaring down on the crowd assembled in the town square to celebrate the wedding. I woke up with a bad feeling this morning, an itch under my skin that won't relent. It goes deeper than my personal feelings. Deeper than the fact that I spent the better part of last night and this morning making sure everything was decorated perfectly for this event.

Pippa Rogers has been my friend since she sat down next to me at lunch on the first day of third grade. We didn't have very much in common, but she was fun, slightly wild, even back then and she drew people to her like a technicolor beacon. While she wasn't the kindest girl in school, she was definitely one who made people pay attention to her.

I saw it happen again and again over the years. Men and women flocked to her side, caught up in her sass, her beauty and her reck-lessness. I tend to watch her through my fingers as though she's a horror movie and I can't be sure when the bad stuff will go down. Pippa is fearless, though, and she never takes anything back. Once it's out there, she might say she's sorry that you're upset by whatever she's said or done, but she *never* apologizes for doing it. What she likes to call living with no regrets I consider pure callousness on her part, but I'm not immune to the pull she has on people. I stand in place across from Raif and his best man, Luke, waiting for Pippa to make her appearance.

Raif looks calm. Calmer than I feel inside anyway. His blonde hair shines golden in the sunlight and is perfectly coiffed, lying flat for once, combed back from his tanned forehead in a sort of mohawk-pompadour hybrid. His short beard is trimmed and neat, his blue-green eyes are bright. The sight of him in his gray suit makes my chest tighten with emotion I don't want to inspect too closely right now. He's tall, broad shouldered, and trim. He's perfection in my eyes. I shoot him a grin, trying to distract myself from worrying about his bride to be and the way my insides are quaking, and he smiles back at me. Longing shoots through me and I tamp it down, trying to ignore the way my body heats in reaction to him.

Luke's eyes roam my way. His full mouth quirks up at one corner as he winks at me, the silver hoop in his nose glinting in the sun. He looks very handsome today, too. He's taller than Raif, but just as broad. His dark hair is perfectly styled in the same pompadour look as the groom's. His full beard is tidy, his blue eyes sparkling out of his handsome face. His suit matches Raif's, contrasting nicely with his dark hair. The full sleeves of tattoos that adorn his arms are covered except for the mermaid tails that dance on the backs of his hands. My cheeks flush when my eyes meet his, and I look at the ground for a moment to collect myself.

If it wasn't so damned hot outside, it would have been the perfect day for a wedding. Not only is the sun pounding down on us, but the air is thick with humidity, causing my heavy hair to frizz despite the hour I spent trying to tame it with hot rollers earlier. I would have preferred a bun to keep the heavy tresses off my neck, but the bride wouldn't be denied. Speaking of Pippa, she should have been right behind me, but I've been standing up here feeling a bead of sweat trickle down between my breasts inside the pink, strapless nightmare of a dress she forced me into for at least five minutes now. Where the hell is she?

Trying not to fidget, I sneak a glance down the aisle in time to see Pippa step into sight on her father's arm. Finally. I let out a slow breath and affix my brightest smile to my face. *Please let her be in this for real*, I beg silently. I can watch her marry the only man I've ever loved if she'll make him happy and truly loves him. No one will ever be the wiser. I gave up hoping for him to look at me romantically long ago. I try not to hope for things I know I can never have.

The hoping hurts too much when it inevitably erodes, leaving me feeling emptier than I began.

My eyes stay glued on Pippa so I won't look at Raif. She's stunning in a knee-length white gown and three-inch heels. Her red hair flames against her bare shoulders in curls that brush the bodice of her gown. She had vetoed a veil and is instead wearing a glittery tiara making her look like a princess from a story book.

She doesn't look happy, though, and I swallow down a knot of unease that tries to crawl up my throat. Her dark blue eyes hold no sparkle. There is no joy in her pretty face, only trepidation. She looks like she might throw up or bolt at any moment. I sneak a covert glance back at Raif and see that he's gone very still, as though bracing himself for a physical blow. I bite my tongue on a curse and turn my gaze back to the bride in time to see her step up beside us in front of Reverend Brownell. I take her proffered bouquet, not meeting her eyes. Pippa turns to face Raif, allowing him to take her hands as he holds himself taut as a wire, ramrod straight.

Reverend Brownell smiles benevolently at all of us and raises his arms, including the entire congregation in his gesture and intones, "Welcome everyone to this joyous occasion." He pauses to look around, takes a breath but Pippa speaks up before he can continue.

Her eyes are glued to Raif's face as she murmurs, "I can't do this." She pulls her hands from his grip and flees, running through the grass in her three-inch heels. I stand there for a moment, blinking, shocked and then look to my best friend to find he's not even surprised. His normally mobile face is shuttered, grim.

I straighten and say, "I'll be right back," to him, kick off the ridiculous shoes she made me wear, and take off running after her. I try calling her name, but she doesn't even flinch. How she's outrunning me in those shoes, I have no idea, but I feel my irritation with her grow.

I put on a burst of speed and manage to snag her elbow in my hand, and she cries out, "No, Chloe, let me go!" I pull with all my might to try and stop her.

"Damn it, Pippa. Knock it off. Talk to me. What the hell are you doing?" I'm winded, chest heaving, dangerously close to losing this damn strapless dress.

She tries to wrench herself free of my hold.

"I just can't do it, okay?" She's trembling all over, but her voice is cold, and I feel my mouth gape open. "Why does it matter to you?" She snaps at me and I feel my control over my temper break.

"You proposed to *him*, Pippa. You insisted it had to be soon, it had to happen now. And now you're walking away." I shake my head at her, my disgust clear in my tone and stance. "You will lose him this time, you know that, right? You can't keep stringing him along this way. It's just not fair and I'm through being quiet about it, damn it. He deserves better than this!"

I knew she wouldn't go through with this, knew she'd never actually marry Raif. Even though she's been swearing up, down and sideways for the last six weeks that she wants to. When you come right down to it, Pippa isn't exactly the marrying type. I never could figure out what possessed her to ask him to begin with.

Yes, you did, a little voice in the back of my head argues, *she was afraid she was going to lose him for good this time and she went all in to avoid that.* I look her up and down, she looks cool and haughty, even now as her mouth works soundlessly, and her eyes fill with big fake tears. I drop her elbow like she's diseased and step back from her.

"You leave him alone from now on, you hear me? I'm done letting you hurt him." My voice is hard and cold, brooking no argument, but her jaw tightens, and she stares me down with her big blue eyes.

7

"Finally ready to admit you've wanted him for yourself all along, Chloe?" Her voice is cold, dangerous and I raise my chin. Maybe I have wanted him, but I've never made a move to get in her way. I've never tried to keep her from him even when I thought she was bad for him. And I have to live with that now, knowing how badly this will hurt him.

"No, Pippa. Just ready to tell you what a manipulative bitch you are and protect him like I should have been doing all along. If you leave him now, don't you dare come back." I say, turning away without waiting to see how she reacts.

"Why would I come back?" She shouts it at my back, but I don't turn around. There's no point in carrying this further.

She'll leave, she doesn't care about Raif, about how much this will hurt him. She's never cared about anyone but herself and I am through making excuses for her and allowing her to walk all over me, make a fool out of Raif. I walk back to the town square, to where Raif is waiting with half the town. He needs me now.

2

Raif

I MIGHT BE IN SHOCK. PIPPA, WHO PROPOSED TO ME, WHO begged me to marry her as soon as possible, is walking away. Well, no, she's running actually. And Chloe is chasing her down. How the fuck did this become my life?

"Dude. You're better off." Luke says, pulling me from my thoughts. His blue eyes are hard on Pippa's back as Chloe chases after her.

I should stop her. There's no point, I know it. I've known it for days, maybe longer. That this just wasn't going to happen, but I kept hoping because Pippa kept insisting she wanted this. She wanted me. I should've known better. *Fucking fool*, a voice echoes in my head. I shake my head at Luke and look out over the crowd of whispering townspeople. My mom looks murderous. She's never liked

9

Pippa to begin with, but the bitching will most likely not stop anytime soon now. Not this time. Mom won't be able to stay silent. And the town will be talking for weeks.

"Fuck." I mutter under my breath. Luke nods his dark head and says simply, "Yep. She's done it this time. Chloe might tear her eyes out."

I sigh at his jovial tone. I know he hates Pippa, he always has. He took one look at her and said, "Raif, she's the devil," in a purely conversational tone. He was nine. I should have listened.

We both watch the girls face off a few dozen feet away, the angry set of Chloe's shoulders, Pippa's cool indifference, and Luke sighs. I have no idea what to do now. Do I tell everyone to go home? Do I stand here like a chump while my best friend tries to convince my fiancé that she wants to marry me? Or can I get really drunk now and possibly forget all about this nightmare? I'd really like to just be left alone. Chloe and Luke could come, of course, but no one else. Everyone else will have half smirks on their faces, eyes full of fake pity. I'm so tired suddenly. I'm seized by the desire to simply curl up on the ground and go to sleep.

Chloe turns from Pippa then, coming back towards me, and I notice she's barefoot, her pretty face stormy. Pippa shouts at her back, but she's looking at me. Why would I come back she asks, and I shake my head, why indeed? I clench my jaw tight, let my gaze drop to the ground. *Stupid*, my head shouts at me. *You knew better. You knew she wasn't right for you. You deserve this. You deserve all of it.*

Then Chloe is back in front of me, angry, not sad and she turns to the front row of spectators where Pippa's parents are sitting looking dumbfounded. She plants her hands on her slim hips, and says, not unkindly, "She's your mess. You can clean this up."

She takes a moment to have a whispered conversation with my mother and younger sister, Daisy. I can't hear what she's saying, but my mother looks slightly less murderous. Mom nods and gets to her feet, taking Daisy's arm. Then they're both walking away while I watch stupidly.

Chloe turns to Luke and me, standing there looking adorable in the strapless pink dress, I know she hates, and says to me, "C'mon, cupcake, this isn't our circus. Let's get out of here." She holds her hand out to me and I take it without hesitation, as I have every time she's ever made the gesture. She tangles our fingers together and murmurs so only I can hear her, "You're gonna be okay, Raif." I know she wouldn't lie to me. Not ever. But I can't help but wonder if she's right as she tugs me away from the wreckage of my non-wedding.

Luke, Chloe and I are now locked inside the calm of The White Oak Saloon or Merle's as it's more affectionately known to the locals. It's Chloe's place, was her granddaddy's before he passed on a few months ago. Chloe, brilliant girl that she is, locked the door and closed all the blinds when we came in. She knows that people know me well enough to know that I'll be hiding in my second home with my favorite people. And sure enough there've been several knocks on the front door. Chloe's ignored them all. I felt bad that she wasn't opening the bar up like usual until I remembered she'd planned on being closed this evening anyway to host my wedding reception.

Luke is seated next to me at the scarred but gleaming bar, his suit jacket tossed carelessly on the bar next to him. His bow tie is gone, his dark hair messy from him raking his fingers through it. Otherwise, he looks like he does any other time we sit in these same seats while Chloe works. I'm still dressed as I was when Chloe towed me away from the town square. I feel numb inside. And a little relieved if I'm being honest. The Jack Daniels is helping me not feel anything at all, though.

When we arrived, Chloe set down coasters at our usual seats, brought out two glass tumblers filled with ice, a bottle of Jack and a two-liter bottle of coke. Then she poured a Guinness for Luke and disappeared into the office behind the bar. A moment later, the central air kicks on, the voice of Johnny Cash singing *Ring of Fire* fills the bar, and I start drinking.

Five minutes later, Chloe emerges behind the bar in denim cut offs and a black tank top. Her feet in flip flops and her thick, dark hair, which had been curled and had tiny pink rosettes pinned in it as it hung down her back, pulled up in a high ponytail. The flowers are all long gone, but the curls remain. I'm betting the pink dress is in the trash bin somewhere in the back, never to be seen again. She left the high heeled shoes she hated in the square. I snort at the recollection causing her to look up at me, alarm clear on her face.

"What's so funny, cupcake?" She asks me, bending down behind the bar and coming back up with a bowl of peanuts and then pretzels. "Eat something, please. I'd prefer you not pickle yourself." She looks pointedly at the still full bottle of soda and the much emptier whiskey one.

"Not drunk." I mumble back at her, but I shove a few pretzels in my mouth to appease her. Most men would take exception at being called cupcake, I know, but it's something I must stand without complaint. Brought it on myself when we were watching Grease one wintery evening in our teens and Frenchie's date to the dance called her a beautiful blonde pineapple or some such nonsense. Chloe looked at me all put out and said, "Why do men insist upon calling women food names?"

Being young and stupid, I didn't realize the best course of action was to say I have no idea and agree that Frenchie's date was a putz.

Instead I said, "Oh, it's not as bad as all that. I wouldn't mind someone calling me cupcake or something like that." And the nickname was born. I cannot—*will* not—tell her she was right. Never. So, I get called cupcake a lot now.

Luke chuckles. "Oh, brother, yes, you are. But it's okay." He takes another swallow of his Guinness, I don't know if that's still his first or if there've been more. He sighs, checking his watch. He looks up at Chloe, "You need me to take him home later?"

He sounds sober. It hasn't been that long, maybe an hour. I've only had a few shots. I eye the half-empty whiskey bottle and think again about the number. I haven't been keeping track. I don't want to think because once I start, inevitably my brain will betray me, and Pippa will be there waiting to eviscerate me.

Chloe comes around the bar with a bottle of water and sits down on the stool next to mine. *How Not to* by Dan + Shay starts playing and I groan, not wanting to hear the song that has always reminded me of Pippa's and my relationship. Chloe rests her tiny hand on my arm, comforting me and looks at Luke. "I've got him covered for the night, don't you worry. If there's somewhere you have to be, it's okay. We'll be fine."

Luke holds Chloe's green eyes for a moment and then sighs, almost sounding wistful. I shake my head at myself. That can't be right. Sure, they dated for a few months, back in high school, but that's been over for ages. They've been friends ever since, never any awkwardness between them. Maybe I am drunk. "I'll only be a phone call away if you need me, sweet tart."

She smiles sweetly at him. "I know you are, Luke. Troy's picking you up?" Everything Chloe does is sweet in my opinion. She's one of those purely goodhearted people that God put here to help the rest of us keep our shit together. Or so I'm convinced. I take another shot of whiskey absently as I watch them.

Luke shakes his head. "I'mma walk it. Troy's found himself a date." Of course he has, Troy could walk into a convent and leave with dates for the next week lined up.

Chloe's eyes flash. "No way. I'll call Bran to come pick you up. You are not walking, you're not exactly steady." He opens his mouth to argue but she cuts him off. "Don't even try it. I know you, Luke Benson. You will sit on that stool until someone comes to collect you or *I* will bring you home later."

I chuckle. "Don't bother arguing, brother. You know our Chloe doesn't play around with people's safety."

He cuts me a look I can't read and says to her, "Don't you have enough to be getting on with here without worrying about me, too?"

She huffs out an exasperated breath at him. "Like I'd be able to relax not knowing if you'd managed to meander your way to your place and not into a ditch somewhere."

Luke snorts at her. "Chloe, love, this is White Oak, there are no ditches." He tilts his head to the side, clearly considering his next word. "I'd be more likely to find my way into the lake, but not a ditch."

She glares at him, and I duck my head, so I'm not caught in the crossfire any longer. I rest my head on the bar, letting my eyes fall closed. I hear Luke say, "Okay, don't look at me like that. One of these days you're gonna turn someone to stone with the power of your mind. I don't want you feeling all that guilt over little old me."

Chloe's clearly trying to hide laughter from her voice when she says, "You just hush, Luke."

She rests her hand on the top of my head before running her fingers over my hair and I sigh at the touch. I hear her moving away from me and despair tugs at me. I want her to come back. I like having her next to me, touching me. But I open my eyes and watch her move around to the other side of the bar. She ducks down, coming back up with another bottle of water. She hands it to Luke.

"Drink that and sit still." She's rocking her Mom voice today. I watch her through my lashes as she pulls out her phone and starts texting.

A few minutes later she tells Luke, "Bran will be here in ten to bring you home. You stay in when you get there, you hear me?"

Luke sighs sadly. "You are just no fun, sweet tart." He downs his water and pushes the empty bottle and his empty glass towards her. "Yes, I promise I will stay in once I arrive home. No wandering into anything potentially fun or dangerous for me tonight."

She smiles at him again. "Good, because we kinda like having you around."

She busies herself tidying things up behind the bar and I watch her absently, enjoying the way her body moves with quick efficiency. Everything bounces invitingly as she leans and stretches, putting things away and getting ready to close things up. I sit up to take another shot and see Luke's watching her, too.

He shakes himself when he catches my eye, and asks, "Rehearsal at two tomorrow, right?"

I nod. "Yes." Pippa and I weren't planning on a honeymoon since she knew the band was booked solid for the next few months. I reach for the whiskey again and notice that Chloe has taken it away and there's a bottle of water in front of me now. I pout, but she's at the other end of the bar and I sigh, defeated. I twist the bottle open and take a long pull before I say, "You'll remind Brandon?"

Luke stretches as he stands when there's a beep outside. "Yep. Troy, too." He claps a hand on my shoulder. "You let Chloe take care of you, okay? We'll see you in the barn tomorrow."

Chloe comes around the bar to hug Luke goodbye. I notice the way his hand rests on the back of her head, pressing her face into his chest, as he drops a kiss to the top of her head. Something shifts in my chest uncomfortably, but I can't put my finger on why. "Holler if you need anything."

Chloe grins up at him, "I will." She walks with him to the front door where she opens it to let him out. I hear her thank Brandon, and once she's sure Luke's safely ensconced in Bran's truck, she comes back in and locks the door behind herself. I'm surprised to see the sun is going down outside. I had no idea we'd been holed up here that long. I look up and see Chloe is standing in front of me, her full mouth turned down on one side as she studies my face.

"What is it?" I ask, reaching out to catch a stray curl that's escaped her ponytail, rubbing the silky strands through my fingers and forcing her to take a step closer. I like her closer. I'm not supposed to, and I try to hide it usually because she's too fine, too good for me to sully. I let my other hand move to her hip and pull her so she's standing between my knees, my back to the bar now. She smells like sunshine to me, always has. Her green eyes are huge and hooked on mine, looking like she thinks I might be crazy.

"What are you doing, Raif?" She asks softly, her voice practically a whisper. Her small hands are on my chest, just resting there and I want them on my skin. I want her. It's a fact I try hard to hide most of the time. From Pippa, from myself, from the whole world. No more Pippa, though. And I'm so tired of wanting her and denying myself.

"I'm just touching your hair, it's soft." I say, trying to downplay how badly I want to pull her even closer, taste her mouth, claim some of that sweetness for myself.

She relaxes a little, her hand moving to my cheek, and then feathering my hair off my face. "You are drunk, cupcake. Want to bunk with me upstairs tonight?"

I hold back a groan when her hand touches my face, nod at her question. "I'd be much obliged."

I release her hair, letting my fingertips trail over her bare shoulder and down her arm, my other hand still gripping her hip. I see a delicate shiver run over her and I give in to the devil on my shoulder and pull her right up against me, her body soft and warm. I drop my head and kiss her shoulder softly, like a whisper against her skin. Her head moves to the side and I move my mouth over her skin, towards the bend of her neck. The tantalizing curve there teases me, and I taste her skin, hear her sharp intake of breath. I keep going, moving up to her ear where I whisper, "I want you."

I feel a moan tremble through her. She turns her head as her body arches into mine, as though without her permission. Her hands fist in my hair. "You don't know what you're saying right now, Raif." Her voice shakes, she's breathless already. I can tell she feels it too, this pull between us.

I cup her cheek in my hand, running my thumb over her mouth, holding her green gaze captive. "I do," I insist. "I've wanted you forever, Chloe. Please.... It doesn't have to go anywhere. Just give me tonight."

Something I don't understand passes through her eyes in a flash and then she leans in and presses her lips to mine. It's a soft kiss. Tentative; but it sparks the need that's been simmering in me, just for her. Need that I've felt for far too long. I lick the seam of her lips and when she parts them I slip my tongue inside to explore her mouth. Her mouth is pliant under my own, her hands clutching my shoulders while I take my time memorizing her taste and every crevice of her perfect mouth.

I stand up off my stool, my mouth only inches from hers, with the intention of putting Chloe on the stool so she's more comfortable. But I stumble.

Her eyes go from dazed to alert in two seconds flat. Her body straightens under my hands. She looks worried now. "Are you okay?"

"I'm fine, I swear. Come back." I wheedle.

Her voice is firm, though, all traces of the lust she seemed to be feeling before gone. Maybe I was wrong? "You *are* drunk," she says, and I can't pinpoint the tone in her voice. "Come on, let's get you upstairs, Raif."

I want to argue. I want to insist that I am fine, and I want *her*. I want her right now before she can talk herself out of it. But one look at her pretty face tells me it would be pointless. She's come back to her senses. Instead I simply nod and let her lead me up the stairs like I'm an old man. I should've known better than to think anything was going to happen between us. She's bound to know she's way too good for the likes of me.

Chloe

WHEN I WAKE THE NEXT MORNING, RAIF IS ALREADY GONE. I feel shame color my cheeks when I recall his kiss from the night before. He was clear that it wouldn't have meant anything. Thank God nothing actually happened. Just some kissing, no big deal. We'll be fine. We came to our senses before any real damage had been done.

That fills me with a bone-achingly deep sense of sadness. The only way he'd want to be physical with me is if it was just one night. At least I know for sure now. Raif and I will never be anything more than friends. I can accept that. No problem. And the moon is made of cream cheese. I sigh at myself. I need to get moving and get the saloon up and running for the day. We lost a whole day and night's worth of revenue thanks to Pippa and it will hurt when it comes time to pay the bills later in the month. But Raif needed his privacy and I needed to at least pretend I could help him feel better. It's not like him to just disappear this way but I try not to examine that too closely. We'll be fine. We have to be.

Less than an hour later, I'm downstairs setting up for the day to come. I basically grew up in this building. Whenever my grandparents could sneak me away from my mother, I was here. I helped them fill napkin dispensers to earn pocket money; danced in the corner in front of the stage while country music played on the jukebox. When I think about home, this place is what springs to mind. That's why I stayed in my apartment upstairs after Merle passed away. This is where we spent our time together, where I still feel them both looking down on me.

The interior is designed like something from an old western movie; the classic saloon doors that swing in and out, hardwood floors that always end up coated in peanut shells at the end of the night. An assortment of battered old cowboy hats and boots are hung on the walls along with black and white pictures of movie cowboys and classic country music stars.

Behind the bar, there's framed photos of me when I was younger, of my grandparents on their wedding day, the day they opened this place. There's one single picture of my mother when she was a child. Her tangle of dark hair falls to the middle of her back, oversized pink sunglasses are perched on her nose as she poses with her hands on her hips in a plastic kiddie pool. She looks happy, carefree. I've never seen her look like that in my lifetime.

When I was younger, before I learned that my mother didn't love anyone. Not even herself. Before, though, I'd spend hours thinking up ways to make her like me, want to spend time with me. Everything from being on my best behavior to cleaning up the house after her and her boyfriends. I tried everything I could think of, but nothing ever worked. As I got older, I stopped trying. Instead, I focused on staying out of her house as often as possible.

My staff should begin arriving soon and then I can try and find Raif and attend to a few errands I've been putting off. Every spare moment I've had for the last two weeks has been devoted to helping with the wedding that didn't happen. Without giving myself time to change my mind, I shoot a quick text message to Luke asking if he's seen Raif today. It's still early for Luke to be up and about after drinking the night before, so I try not to stress when he doesn't immediately respond as he normally would.

I stare at my phone like an idiot for a few moments, waiting for it to do something. Anything would do, even a measly emoticon text letting me know he's alive. I shake myself after a full two minutes of silent communion with my empty screen, I have things to do, damn it. I am not normally this neurotic. I force the wedding, Raif, and our disastrous kiss out of my head and get to work, determined not to dwell on any of it right now.

The problem with trying to put it out of my head is that Raif has been a huge part of my life for as long as I can remember. When we were kids and my mother would get black-out drunk or high and forget to cook or food shop, I would turn up at Raif's back door and he would sneak me snacks. That was when his father was still around, so we had to hide it from the adults. Then in high school when my mother brought her new men around at night and I didn't feel safe, I'd sneak out my window. Violet Montgomery grew accustomed to coming in to wake her son up for school and finding me cuddled up with him.

Pippa didn't like it, but Raif was my safe place. He was the one who had always been there when my doorknob rattled at night and I felt fear creep into my chest. Or when my mother came home high and decided she didn't want me around to distract her boyfriends. I could never confide in Pippa about my mother and the way she lived. Raif knows, though, he's seen it all. Just like I'd been there to clean up his injuries after beatings from his father.

Pippa didn't know about any of that, though. She wasn't good at going beyond the surface of things. Her life was easy, picture perfect, and she didn't really take the time to see that wasn't so for Raif or me. Either way, Pippa would never say anything to Raif about her true feelings. She felt no such reluctance with me. She'd snarled at me to stay away from her man many times when he was out of earshot and then reverted to her sweeter self when he returned. I kept my mouth shut, seeing her insecurity for what it was, but I refused to be run off.

Luckily, the morning waitress, Zora, comes gliding in to distract me. Zora's bright smile is affixed in place, her light brown eyes alive with curiosity. I know without a doubt that she's about to grill me for details on what happened with Raif and Pippa. I realize that this is what I can look forward to wherever I go for the foreseeable future. Or I can just barricade myself in the saloon and let them all come here and spend money before they interrogate me. Either way, I have nothing to say to any of them. I don't tell my friends' business, even if one of them has pissed me off so badly I never want to see her again and the other has me twisted in knots after one ill-conceived kiss.

"Morning, gorgeous," Zora says, tying her apron around her narrow waist after she stows her purse in the office. "You got all the wedding decorations down already." She looks around, clearly surprised I've been so efficient while dealing with Raif's jilting.

"I had some time yesterday." I say, as I take chairs down off the tables. She switches the jukebox on and starts from the far side of the room, doing the same.

"How's Raif doing?" She asks, studiedly nonchalant as she works.

I shoot her a withering glance. "He'll be fine."

She sighs, then changes tactics. "I can't believe Pippa walked away from him." Clearly, she thinks if she abuses Pippa, I'll cave and give her gossip to spread. She'll never learn.

"Move on, Zora. You know I'm not telling tales."

"But, Chloe, you actually know what happened. C'mon, give me something. Was there someone else? *I* heard that she's been screwing Deputy Stover. Marjorie over at Munchies, she said she saw them out in his cruiser behind the station the other night." She pauses in her storytelling to watch my face as I continue taking the chairs down. I try to keep my face blank. There've been rumors that Pippa sleeps around for ages, but I've never engaged with anyone who told me tales. Pippa knew better than to let me find out if any of it was ever true.

I know too well how it feels to be the subject of the stories being spread around town by the general public. It's one of the drawbacks to living in a small town, where everyone knows everyone else and thinks they know all there is to know about you. I won't be a part of tearing anyone else down.

Taking down the last chair, I turn to face her head on. "Zora, remember all those other times I gossiped with you about other people's business?"

Her full mouth tilts down. "That's cuz you're no fun, boss." She sighs, clearly disgusted with me. "Well, whatever—you tell Raif I'm here to comfort him *anytime*."

My face flushes and my jaw clenches. "I'll be sure to pass that along," I manage dryly. I swallow and nod towards the back. "Can you turn the grill on for Odetta? She should be here any moment." Zora nods and scampers off to do as I asked, leaving me with my muddled thoughts.

I don't want to think of Raif with anyone new. It was hard

enough to watch him with Pippa. But I suppose it's inevitable that he'll find someone new and temporary. Rebound and all that. Is that what I would have been for him last night, I wonder? A rebound one-night stand with someone he could trust? The thought sends pain lancing through me. I wish I'd never kissed him. We could've laughed this off if I hadn't been so weak. But no, he'd been so close and solid and warm. Sexy as sin and safe as houses right there in front of me. I'd been able to see the lust in his eyes. And I'd fallen.

Stupid. Stupid. Stupid.

I keep myself busy setting up and I hear, rather than see Odetta come in for her shift. She and Zora chat together happily in the kitchen. The two are opposites physically—Zora young and fit, care-free with skin the rich color of a mocha latte and curly dark hair that bounces all on its own. Odetta refuses to tell anyone her age, dyes her hair a bright flame red and is as pale as milk. Her eyes are sky blue and her thin mouth spends most of its time frowning. Her smiles are rare, but I think she's just generally disappointed by life. She's everyone's surrogate mother and has worked here since my granny died when I was twelve. I always thought she had a soft spot for my granddaddy, but nothing ever came of it. Probably because Merle Morris never got over the death of Delilah, his wife and only love.

I flip the open sign on, listening to the neon hum and glance around to make sure we're ready for customers. We have our regulars who'll be in for lunch. This town is as predictable as they come. No one likes to mess around with the status quo. One more reason they'll be talking about Pippa and Raif for weeks to come. They all need to get a life in my opinion. But I don't rock the boat if I can help it. The town has enough fun talking about my mother, and I can feel the weight of their low expectations of me. Half of them are convinced I'll end up just like her.

Hank Warner is our first customer of the day, just like every other day. He's been retired from the insurance business for two years now and he seems to be determined to keep himself in a routine, so he doesn't go senile from lack of things to do. More importantly, he is a sucker for Odetta's cooking and town gossip. Every day he lets Odetta pick what she feeds him. I'm about to head into the office to look at the books since Zora has things well in hand for the time being when the door opens again, and Lilly May Morris comes stumbling inside. *Wonderful.*

My mother isn't supposed to come here, she's been banned since before I was born. She's only attempted to break this once before since my grandfather died, and that was at the gathering I held here after his funeral—which she did not attend. I don't have bouncers on staff until later in the day and I won't make Zora deal with this.

My mother looks to be on the backend of a bender. She's wearing a ratty old black negligee, her feet balancing precariously on sandals with three-inch stiletto heels. Her dark hair is stringy and hanging limply around her face, a tangled mess. I can smell her from across the room—stale sweat, sex, booze, and cigarette smoke.

She's looking around. What she's searching for I have no idea, but I really don't need this hassle today. I wait until I'm right in front of her to speak so as not to create a bigger scene.

"You know you're not supposed to be here." I warn her, and finally her grey eyes fix on me. She looks haggard, dazed, like she's surprised to find me here.

"This is my daddy's place, and I'll come here whenever I want." Her voice is loud, her words slurred.

I grab onto her bony elbow and attempt to steer her back outside, keeping my voice low but firm. "No. It's not. It's mine. Merle died, Lilly. Remember? And even before that, he didn't allow you in here. Time to go."

She gets louder, jerking her elbow out of my grasp and causing herself to stumble back a few steps and then fall unceremoniously to the floor. "I don't know who you think you are, but I have just as much right to this place as you do!" Her over mascaraed eyes bore into mine, as she tries to draw me into her game. I am not the one who enjoys making a public spectacle every time she leaves the house. I am not this person. I won't be. The town can tell their tales about someone else tonight.

I step back from her, pulling my cell phone out of my apron. I dial the numbers quickly while my mother glares up at me from her undignified sprawl on the floor. When the phone is answered on the second ring, I say, "This is Chloe Morris over at the Saloon, can you send the sheriff over please? I have an intruder upsetting my customers."

Then I turn, and keeping my head held high, I return to the office, leaving my mother to play out her drama alone.

Raif

I'M A FUCKING COWARD. I WOKE UP ON THE PULLOUT COUCH IN Chloe's apartment with the mother of all hangovers. I've crashed there enough to not be disoriented while I blinked around blearily. My gaze caught on a framed photo of Chloe and me from the previous summer when she'd accompanied the band to an outdoor music festival. My arm is slung casually around her shoulders, her dark hair pulled back in a messy ponytail, her pretty face alight with laughter. She looks carefree—we both do. And I most likely ruined everything wanting things I know I don't deserve. I looked around the familiar space, the weight of what we might have done settling on my shoulders like a heavy cloak. My stomach rolled over in abject terror at the thought of losing her friendship. And I bolted.

I walk to my mother's house in the early morning light, avoiding

27

the small house on Peach Street that Pippa and I had rented. I have no idea if she's there, or if just her belongings are taking up residence. I'm not ready to find out yet. The town is silent this early in the morning. Even with my stomach churning and my head pounding, I can't help but appreciate the quiet beauty of the tree lined streets where I grew up.

The walk from the Saloon is short. Four blocks from the town square, I turn onto Plum Street and jog up the steps to the fourth house on the left. I avoid looking at the rundown building to the right of it. The house where Chloe grew up. Lilly May hasn't lived there in ages now. Not since Chloe left to live above the Saloon right after she turned eighteen. I can feel the memories lurking at the edges of my mind, there to remind me of what I might have lost last night. All due to my own stupidity.

Mom isn't surprised when I let myself in. She's alone in the dining room, her light blue robe wrapped tight around her slim frame. "You look like hell," she greets me, and I shoot her a tired grin.

"Love you, too, Ma. I guess being left at the altar doesn't agree with me."

She nods at the empty chair across from her at the dining table. "Sit. I want to talk to you."

I flop gracelessly into the too small chair and reach for a cup off the lazy susan in the middle of the table. The stainless-steel urn perched in the center of the console scents the room with strong coffee and I pour myself a cup, inhaling the fumes reverently. Today will most likely require a lot of coffee if I'm going to make it through rehearsal this afternoon. I take a gulp of the scalding liquid and then finally meet my mother's worried blue eyes. "I'm fine," I say, before she can start.

She sighs at me. "Oh, don't bother lying. There's no shame in being upset she did this, Raif."

I hold her eyes for a beat and shrug halfheartedly. "I don't know who I'm angrier with, really." I confide. "I was almost *relieved* when she stalked off. I don't think I loved her the way I should've to marry her. And if that's the case, what kind of man does that make me?" I stare into the swirling darkness in my coffee cup. I feel my mom's smaller hand come around mine and she squeezes gently.

"Doesn't mean it doesn't hurt that she dragged your heart and your reputation through the mud in this town for the last decade. I've known for a while you didn't love her like you should, but I wasn't going to tell you what to do."

I feel heat in my cheeks, but I don't dispute the facts. She's right. Word around town is that Pippa has been sleeping around for years. I try to ignore the gossips, but I couldn't help but believe them. Still, every time she came back to me after we'd split up, I ignored the voice in my head that told me to cut her loose and start over with someone new. She was what I knew. She was what I felt I deserved. Really, this is all my fault when it comes right down to it. I was using her as surely as she was me.

I look up to meet my mom's eyes. "I'll be okay, Mom. You don't have to worry."

She doesn't sound convinced of that. "I know you, son. And I love you, but for some reason, you keep letting her come back and do this to you over and over again. So, I'm telling you now that you need to man up and cut her out of your life. Don't let her back in. Especially if you don't love her, Raif." Her voice is as serious as I've ever heard it. I open my mouth to reply, but she continues. "You deserve to be happy, Raif." I hear the sadness and worry for me in her voice. "I know things that happened with your father left their mark." She winces at her choice of words. I nod to let her know I heard her, unable to speak for the moment.

That part of me that remembers the dark days before my

mother divorced the sonofabitch who fathered my sister and me tries to lock the memories down before they can rear up and nut punch me. It never works, though. I was six the first time I saw my father beat my mother. She'd burned dinner because she was busy trying to feed Daisy, who was only six months old at the time. I watched in horrified silence as my father grabbed my mother by the hair and slammed her head off the kitchen wall then proceeded to try and force feed her the scorched mashed potatoes she'd served at dinner.

I intervened, not thinking about the fact that my father was bigger, drunk and obviously angry. I didn't think it through, I just launched my small, bony body against his legs and tried my best to get him off my mother. For my trouble, my father kicked me across the room, making my mother scream around the food he kept shoving in her mouth. I tried again, even though I was hurt, limping across the room to pummel him with my ineffectual fists. He hit me across the face that time, knocking me back to the floor on my back, the room going fuzzy when my head cracked hard against the hardwood floor.

My mother says my name, squeezing my hand hard to bring me out of the memories. It certainly wasn't the last time it happened. She didn't divorce him until he put me in the hospital when I was ten.

Luke finds me behind the house an hour before we're due at Bran's family's farm for rehearsal. I'm coated in sweat from pulling weeds. Mom said it's therapeutic, but I think she just wanted me out from underfoot. I have trouble sitting still when something's on my mind.

"Well, this looks like fun." Luke says by way of greeting. I look back at him, wiping my forehead across my arm to get some of the sweat out of my eyes.

"Yeah. Just trying to help Mom." I tell him, turning back to my task.

"You lose your phone?" Luke asks, settling down next to me to help. There's an edge to his normally amiable tone, something sharp like I've pissed him off. Which is insane because Luke doesn't get pissed off. He's the most even-tempered person I know.

I glance over at him to find his face impassive as he pulls out weeds from the bed of geraniums. "No, it was dead when I got home earlier. Charger's at the new place and I'm not going there."

Luke's shoulders relax a little. "Ah, yes. Well, don't worry. Word is Pippa's been shipped out west to visit her grandmother. And Chloe called her parents earlier and they got all her stuff out of your place. So, it's safe."

I drop my head, feeling ashamed that once again my best friend is taking care of me. "She didn't have to do that." I mutter.

Luke snorts. "She doesn't *have* to do half the shit she does for us. But you can't stop her." He sighs. "If you want to thank her, you could use my phone and call her, she's worried about you. Says you left without saying goodbye."

"Fuck." I mutter. "I didn't mean to worry her. I'll call her after rehearsal."

Luke's silent for a moment, beheading a few geraniums as he tugs up the weeds. When he speaks next, his voice has that sharp edge again. "Did something happen last night? She seemed upset..."

I study my portion of the geraniums like they hold the secrets to the universe, working to keep my face blank. "No, I don't think so. I was drunk, she took care of me. I just woke up in a snit and took off." I shrug, trying to pass off a nonchalance I don't feel. "I'll talk to her after."

Luke makes a noncommittal sound in his throat. "Well, alright then." He beheads a few more geraniums and asks, "How are you doing with everything?" His voice is softer now. More gentle than usual and I groan in response.

"Brother, I know you mean well, I do. Honestly, though, I don't want to talk about it. I'm not heartbroken over Pippa leaving. And that makes me a pretty disgusting person, so...I'll keep you posted if anything changes. But for right now, I just want to pull some weeds and then go play some music for a while. Get ready for our set at the Saloon tomorrow night."

Luke holds my eyes for a beat and then nods. "Alright then, brother. Whatever you say."

Chloe

Saturdays are always hectic at the saloon, our busiest day of the week. I should be occupied enough to not dwell on the fact that it's been almost two whole days since I last saw Raif. But I'm not. The fact that he didn't call me, merely sent me a short text message the previous evening letting me know he was okay does not help my peace of mind. Normally, he'd call. Raif loathes texting, he thinks it's impersonal and borderline rude. I've been in a barely concealed panic since the message came in last night. It's pathetic, really.

I force myself to focus on the crowd where I'm stationed at the bar and not on my disintegrating relationship with my best friend. Or I try to, at least. I'm not very successful, my body might be busy, but my mind whirs with disturbing thoughts and worst-case scenarios. What if we're awkward forever now, and we don't ever get past this whole debacle? What will I do without him? Raif has been my closest friend my entire life, I don't know who I am without him in my life. I don't want to find out.

I'm mixing up a pitcher of margaritas for a table of loud college-aged girls who are home for the summer when I see the boys of Renegades come in the back door. I try to keep my attention on the task in front of me. I don't want to make the drinks too strong. But I know Raif is back there, most likely ignoring my existence for the very first time in our lives. I keep my eyes on the liquor I'm adding, my ears perked for the sound of a familiar deep voice coming to say hello. That would be normal. He doesn't come over, though. I send Zora over to the table with the girls' order and move on to the next customer, my heart aching in my chest.

I fill all the orders, listening as the guys set up, until I have nothing left to do. More unsettled than ever, I seek refuge in the office. I need to get it together before someone notices that I'm unraveling. I sit down behind the desk and let my head fall into my hands. *Woman up, Chloe,* I chide myself silently, *you have to go back out there and pretend that everything's fine.* During my lukewarm pep talk, there's a quiet rap on the office door. *Raif!* my heart squeals, trying to beat its way out of my chest.

"C'mon in." I manage, my pulse thundering in my ears.

The door opens and Luke's dark head pokes inside, making my heart plummet down into my stomach. I keep a smile plastered on my face, though. "Hey, sweet tart, how's it going?" He opens the door wide and steps inside, and behind him, looking like he might be ill at any moment, is Raif. My heart starts pounding again, making me nauseous with the sudden shift.

Trying to calm my heart before I throw up on something, I stand and motion them inside. "Hey boys. What can I do for you?"

Luke comes over and pulls me into a one-armed hug, dropping a kiss on the top of my head. "Well, we saw you leave the bar and wanted to say hi."

I hug him back and grin up at him, "Hello. Yes, I figured I'd hide while I had the opportunity." I step out of Luke's embrace and chance a look up at Raif. He looks lost. Embarrassed. I feel my heartbeat slow to a crawl in my chest. He can't even look at me. My stomach twists and I feel despair crowd in. But I can't let him know I'm upset. I plaster on a huge, fake smile and hug him hard. "Hiya, cupcake. You okay?" I'm proud of myself when my voice doesn't wobble even though I can feel the tears building in my chest.

He's tense at first but after a moment his arms come around me and he crushes me against his broad frame. He buries his face in my hair and murmurs into my ear, so soft I can barely hear him despite his proximity. "I'm so sorry." I feel the shaky breath he expels skitter over my skin. "I missed you," he continues, and I cling tight to him, afraid to reply.

I force the tears back down. No time for them right now. And I don't want him feeling guilty about me. I rub his back, comforting him the only way I know how. I lie. "We're okay." I whisper back to him as my heart splinters in my chest. "I missed you, too."

I can feel Luke's keen eyes on us and I step back from Raif keeping that maniacally huge smile on my face. "Can I get you boys a drink before your set? Or just water like usual?" My voice is a little chipper, but it can't be helped right now. Time to fake it. I'm not giving the town anything else to talk about.

"Water's good," Luke says giving me a look I don't understand. "You want to introduce us, Chlo? Or want us to grab Zora?"

I grin at him, still faking happiness as hard as I can. "Of course, I'm introducing you." I pat his cheek. "This is my place and you're my boys. No one else will *ever* introduce you here."

Luke smiles at me and I feel Raif put a hand lightly on my waist. "Just making sure you were up for it," Luke says, watching me closely.

"Well, you should know better," I sass back at him. "I have half a mind to be insulted by that question."

Raif is silent behind me, his hand like an iron branding my skin through my thin tank, but I focus on Luke and normalcy for now. I glance at the clock and see it's almost eight. "You guys better go finish setting up. You're supposed to start in less than ten minutes."

Luke nods at me still looking concerned, and Raif's hand tightens on me for a moment. Luckily, Luke saves me further humiliation by leading Raif out. "We'll see you in ten," he tells me with his usual good humor. I nod like a bobble head and close the door behind them, resting my forehead against it a moment.

We just can't ever talk about it, I decide. We'll be fine if we pretend it never happened. Nodding to myself, I put my game face on and leave the sanctuary of the office.

For the rest of the night, I keep myself busy as the boys play their hearts out. It's a good set, mostly covers with some original songs thrown in the mix. The crowd loves them, which is nothing new. Renegades is the only local band in White Oak and the boys are talented. I think they're going places, which is why I book them at least twice a month, just like Merle did. I know I'm biased because I'm a de facto manager for them, but most of the time I prefer listening to them over anything that gets played on the radio.

The crowd is loud and active, the dance floor full all night. Luckily, the central air works like a dream, keeping the interior of the saloon comfortable for the patrons. The kitchen closes at midnight, and once she's finished her night time routine back there, Odetta comes out and takes a seat at the bar to watch the last of the boys' performance. I grin, knowing it won't be long before she'll be out on the dance floor. Odetta loves to dance and the younger guys love getting her out on the floor.

The Renegades start up their cover of Garth Brooks' *Ain't Goin' Down til the Sun Comes up* and the crowd goes wild. I watch Odetta tapping her feet and singing along and after a few seconds, Wayne Beale, the sheriff's youngest son, comes up and asks her to dance. He's here with all his friends celebrating his twenty-first birthday and I know Odetta won't turn him down.

Odetta favors him with a rare wide smile and hands me her purse to set behind the bar. I laugh and egg them on. "Go on now, you two. Go show them how it's done."

Odetta waves me off but in a moment, she's out there putting the younger dancers to shame. I have no idea where the woman gets her energy from. I carry on tapping my feet as I wipe down the bar and restock the empty bowls of peanuts and pretzels. The boys will only play one more song, but last call is still hours off. I try and take advantage of every lull in the hectic Saturday pace.

When the song ends, Odetta stays out on the floor. Raif thanks the crowd and then he does something unexpected. "Okay, this is our last song for tonight. You guys have been amazing." I look up to find his eyes locked on mine and my mouth goes dry. "I want to take a moment to send a message out if you'll bear with me, folks." He shoots them his shy grin, the one that I love, the one that plenty of girls have swooned over. I'm still caught in his gaze, even from across the room. "As you know, Chloe Morris is the owner of this fine estab-lishment. Most of you probably also know that she's my best friend. Has been my whole life. I just want to shout out to her tonight and make sure she knows how much I love and appreciate her. She's my rock, and I'd be lost without her. So, this song is for you, Chloe Jane, because I know how much you love it."

They launch into *Lately* by Dan + Shay and I feel tears prick at my eyes. Ridiculous of me, I know, but I know Raif hates it. He associates Dan + Shay with what he calls the pop takeover of true country music. Playing this song is Raif begging me for forgiveness in his own way. Which is ridiculous because we're both adults and it's not his fault that he doesn't love me like I love him. He was drunk and emotionally wrecked and *I* should have stopped him. This is my fault for being selfish.

My thoughts continue to chase each other around inside my head, but I do love this song and after a few moments, I find myself caught in the rich timbre of Raif's voice as he sings it. The music surrounds me, his voice a velvet caress against my skin and I close my eyes against the sting of tears. My chest tightens, my breath lodged in my throat behind the tears I'm holding back, and I feel Zora come up on my side and wrap her arm around my waist. She gives me a quick squeeze, pulling me into her side and resting her head against mine. Like she knows the turmoil I'm feeling inside, how I wish so desperately that he meant the words he's singing.

I shoot Zora a watery grin. "I'm okay." I mumble to her and she nods.

"I know that. Just wanted to squeeze you." She dimples at me and then moves along to fill an order. My face falls a bit once she's out of sight and I battle to force my face into normal lines. I know people are watching me. I can feel their curious eyes roaming over me.

The boys wrap up and before Luke has finished thanking the crowd, Raif is off the stage and coming straight for me. I swallow hard, working to bring moisture into the desert my mouth has become. I untie my apron for something to do and when I look up again, he's standing in front of me behind the bar, blue eyes boring into mine. "Chloe Jane," he says, his voice a gravelly whisper, full of so much pain and regret that it rips at my heart. "I'm so sorry about yesterday." He sounds like he could cry.

He opens his mouth to continue, but I step forward and wrap my arms around his slim waist, needing to comfort him, desperate to stop his next words. If he says anything else, we won't be able to go back. We'll be talking about it and then we'll never be the same. I can't lose him, and I don't want to be one more thing he feels guilty about. I burrow into his chest, clutching him to me. "It's okay, cupcake," I tell him again, cutting him off. "We're okay."

His arms come around me and he grips me like I'm the only thing holding him together. After a moment, I feel the tension leave his body and he sags a bit against me, clasping me tighter to him. I do the same, keeping my face hidden so he can't see anything in my eyes to give me away. And we stay that way for a long moment, his face buried in my neck, hanging onto each other for dear life.

Raif

Six Weeks Later...

Bright summer sunshine is pouring in, blinding me before I even open my eyes for the first time today. I roll over and barely hold back a scream when I tumble to a hard floor. My stomach churns, threatening to return the Jack Daniels I drank for my supper after the show last night. I groan, clutching my head as it spins, attempt to stand up and open my eyes at the same time. That's a mistake. The room whirls dizzyingly, my stomach revolts and I vomit up its contents all over the floor. I sink to the mattress once more, hands braced on my knees, waiting to see if anything else comes up.

I almost jump out of my skin when I hear someone knocking at the door at the same time as a small hand touches my lower back. "You alright, baby?" It's a husky voice, female. I have no earthly idea who it belongs to. I groan again and ignore her.

There's another knock at the door and before I can attempt to get to my feet again, I hear the door opening. "Raif? It's Chloe, are you still in bed?"

That wakes me up. I pull the sheet off the girl in my bed, wrapping it around my waist and meet my best friend in the hallway outside my bedroom. She looks fresh as a spring day, her long dark hair falling loose for once, hitting the small of her back. Her green eyes are wide, traveling the expanse of my naked torso before meeting mine again. Her nose wrinkles as she gets a whiff of me and I obligingly take two steps back from her. "Sorry," I mutter. "I uh-"

"You drank too much last night and were just emptying your guts into the toilet?" she responds with one dark eyebrow quirked.

I grin at her sheepishly. "All over the floor, actually." I sigh. "What can I do for you, Chloe Jane?"

Hurt flickers through her eyes before her gaze drops to the floor and she says, with no emotion in her voice. "You forgot."

My bedroom door opens behind me and I close my eyes, knowing in the pit of my stomach that things are about to get even worse.

"He's busy, sweetheart." The stranger who shared my bed last night declares from right behind me, her cool hand resting on my shoulder. Lisa maybe? Damn it, it doesn't matter. I shrug her off and turn to find her naked. *Super.* Long black hair, big brown eyes, a nice enough body I suppose. I still can't remember her name, though. "You should just run along now."

"Hey now-" I begin, but Chloe cuts me off.

Chloe laughs. "Sure he is, honey. Odds are he doesn't remember your name right now." I frown, my face heating at her words. Chloe shakes her head in my general direction. "I'm guessing we won't be working on any songs today, so I'm gonna go to work." She sounds hurt and maybe even a little pissed off.

"Chloe, wait, I'm sorry." I try, but she's walking away without looking back. The black-haired girl grabs my elbow when I make to follow her. "Let me go." I say without turning around, my voice cold. The girl drops my arm like I might bite her.

"Asshole." She mutters and storms back into my bedroom, slamming the door behind her.

"Chloe!" I yell and manage to catch up to her at the front door. I catch her elbow in my hand, and tug on her gently to stop her from leaving. "Please, wait a minute, Chloe."

Her shoulders come down and she turns around, pulling her elbow out of my grasp and crossing her arms across her chest. She raises her chin and glares up at me. "What?" She asks without inflection, her voice lacking the sweetness it usually carries.

I gulp. "I didn't forget. I just woke up. Don't be angry at me, you know I can't stand it when you're mad at me."

"Do you know how many days off I've taken in the last month, Raif?" She asks, her voice quiet.

"Um. No, probably one or two?" I offer up lamely, trying to make my brain work.

"None. I've taken no days off since you didn't get married." I flinch at her words, but she presses on. "I'm here today because you *begged* me to come and help you write a song for the festival you guys are playing next month. You said you missed me and wanted to hang out and we could kill two birds with one stone. Well, here I am, and you're still drunk from last night."

"I said I'm sorry," I mutter. "I have missed you! Why can't you just hang out for a bit, let me get a shower and then we can get to work?"

Before Chloe can respond, the black-haired girl whose name I still can't remember comes stomping out of my bedroom, dressed now, thankfully. She glares at us, looking pointedly at the door Chloe and I are blocking. Without thinking about it, I wrap my arm around Chloe's waist and pull her towards me, my other hand still holding my sheet around my hips. Chloe comes up against my chest and the girl storms out of the house, slamming the door behind her, making the windows rattle.

Chloe is still staring daggers at me and puts her hands against my chest and pushes me away from her. She's never done that before. She never minded if I touched her. She must really be mad at me.

I frown down at her. "I know I screwed up. I'm sorry." I reach out a hand, intending to touch her face and she swats it away.

Her pretty face is still screwed up in anger. "Don't touch me right now, please. You can't just make this go away." There's something in her voice that I can't figure out; pain or anger? I can't tell. "Go take your shower, I'll put on coffee. You better be ready to work when you get out, Raif. I'm not coddling you anymore. I know things have been hard for you since Pippa took off. But you need to pull it together." Right now, she's echoing what my mother told me two days ago when she cornered me at Munchies where I was having lunch with Daisy. I never expected this.

I nod, hurt by her words. Chloe has told me off countless times over the course of our friendship, but she's never shunned my touch. She never made me feel inadequate, never made me feel useless. I don't like this feeling her words have brought on.

After my shower, I find Chloe has restored some semblance of order to my house. There are no longer empty beer bottles littering my coffee table. No half empty whiskey bottles take up residence on the counters in the kitchen. They're all put away, knowing Chloe. The place even smells better. There's coffee percolating, and the smell of cinnamon emanates from the oven. She's frying eggs when I come upon her in the kitchen.

Her back is to me and I do something I know I shouldn't. I take my time and drink in the sight of her in her denim mini skirt and black tank top. She's all curves and long dark hair tumbling to the small of her back. Her feet are bare on the hardwood floor of my kitchen. She's humming a Mary Chapin Carpenter song, her hips swinging back and forth, toes tapping to the beat. Grinning, I lean against the counter and silently watch her for a moment. She is completely at ease, lost in the song playing in her head. She seems to have lost the tension that was keeping her rigid and out of my reach earlier. Longing shoots through me, and I wonder what she'd do if I walked up behind her right now and pulled her against me.

If her earlier reluctance for my touch is any indication, she might sock me in the mouth. Even if all I want is to hold her. Before I can talk myself out of it, I step up behind her and put my hands on her hips, dancing with her, moving my hips with her rhythm and singing out loud the words she's been humming.

I sing softly in her ear, picking up the song. I feel her shiver, she keeps moving, but her humming has stopped. I wrap my arms around her, pulling her back against my body as we move.

She smells like sunshine, bright and fresh; and the curve where her neck meets her shoulder is taunting me. Our hips are still moving slightly, our bodies pressed close together, and she has to feel how turned on I am by just the nearness of her. The desire to kiss that luscious curve only inches from my lips is building. I lean down, my mouth is about to settle over her skin, and the oven timer goes off, jolting us both. She practically jumps out of my arms, turning the alarm off and then rummaging for potholders.

"Cinnamon rolls are done," she says unnecessarily, not looking at me. I watch her profile, her cheeks are rosy, her chest rising and falling at a slightly rapid rate. She's not unaffected by me. That makes me feel a little better. I move to the refrigerator, hiding my face inside for a moment, trying to get my hormones under control.

"Thanks for cleaning up," I say, bringing out the milk and orange juice, like that was what I'd been after all along. "You didn't have to do that."

Her face is hidden by her long hair. "I didn't mind."

"And the mess was surely making you twitchy." I chuckle when she huffs at me in response.

"Maybe. I figured we'd get more work done if I wasn't worried about what I might sit in." There's a bit more venom in her voice now.

"You got something to get off your chest, Chloe Jane?"

She sighs at me, turns to face me finally and plants her hands on her hips. "I just hope you're being safe about being reckless." There's no anger in her voice now, simply concern. "You're acting a bit more like Troy than yourself lately, cupcake."

I frown, my eyes on the table where she's just put the now iced cinnamon rolls and the eggs. I go to the cupboard and gather plates, silverware, and cups to bring to the table, unsure of what I can even say to defend my recent behavior. She's not wrong. A different girl each night. Because I know I can't have Chloe, and Pippa's gone and what's the point of being good? I brace my hands on the counter and hang my head, ashamed. Is this really what I've become? A moment later, Chloe comes up behind me and lays a hand on my back.

I turn and pull her into my arms, hugging her close. "I'm a mess," I say into her hair.

She pulls back to look up at me, her emerald eyes shining. "Maybe right now, but only you can change it." She's so sincere it hurts to see her hope for me just oozing out of her. I trail my knuckles over her cheekbone, and she swallows, licks her lips.

I don't think about how she deserves better than me. I don't analyze my motives or how she might react. I do what I've been doing for the last month or so, I simply follow my desire. I lean down, watching as Chloe's eyes grow wider, wary as I get closer. I claim her mouth in a heated kiss and her body stiffens in my arms. Nothing like the last time I kissed her when she melted against me. She wrenches her mouth from mine, pushing against my chest to get me to let her go.

"Stop!" She orders finally when I'm too slow to do so. I expect to see anger, or maybe even disgust. But I see hurt there and I feel lower than ever before. She steps back from me and crosses her arms over her chest. I can see that she's shaking. Without thinking twice, I step towards her, but she holds up her hand to halt me.

"I'm sorry." I start but she speaks over me.

"Don't. You're not sorry. You didn't even think about what would happen if you kissed me and you're not drunk. It's not like before. You look at me as just another groupie? I matter that little to you that you'd throw our friendship away for whatever pleasure you could take from an afternoon tryst? You'd give me up?" Her voice is shaking, her green eyes full of tears and I've never been so ashamed of myself. She shakes her head at me, her voice stronger now. "I'm *not* your groupie. I'm supposed to matter more to you than that girl who slunk out of here earlier whose name you don't know."

She swipes her hands across her cheeks, angrily dashing away tears and I've never felt worse. Not until she walks out of my house without once looking back at me that is.

Chloe

I leave Raif's and make my way to the cemetery at the edge of town. I'm still bawling which pisses me off. I hate crying. It's a waste of time, won't change anything. I learned that at a young age. I want to go home and hide in my bed. But I'd pass at least twenty people and have to socialize before I could escape. And then there would be talk. At least if someone sees me here with tears on my face, it will be easier to explain.

I park and make my way to my grandparents' graves. A single gravestone with both their names on it adorns the graves. Fresh pain pierces my heart. I miss them both so much. I feel so alone. I flop down on the ground facing the stone, heedless of the skirt I'm wearing. I pull my knees up and rest my chin on them and let myself cry. I miss my grandparents, yes, but mostly I miss Raif as he was before

Pippa walked out on him. I miss my best friend, the Raif who didn't cross the boundaries of friendship and give me emotional whiplash.

Yes, I've been in love with him for as long as I can remember, but I never acted on it and he never behaved as anything but a friend. There was none of this kissing and borderline dirty dancing. No weird, long looks where he seems to be contemplating gobbling me up. I don't know what to think or feel. Especially since Raif's become so promiscuous. I don't want to be another notch on his bedpost. Just another girl he can fuck and forget about it. I can't ease the hurt in my chest at the thought that I'm disposable to him. One more person who has decided that they don't need me around.

I don't know how long I sit there letting it all out, soaking the front of my skirt with my tears but when I calm down, I realize I'm not alone anymore. I turn and find Luke sitting there, looking off into the distance. "Luke Benson, you're going to give me a heart attack one of these days." I'd sound more intimidating if my voice wasn't thick with tears.

He's sitting on the ground next to me, mimicking my pose. "Sorry, sweet tart. I didn't want to disturb you." He wraps a strong arm around my shoulders and pulls me into his chest. "Tell me all about it, honey. What's going on?"

I allow myself to accept the comfort he's offering, leaning into him and snuggling into his hug. "Bad day." I say, not untruthfully.

He hums a bit, rubbing my back. "Funnily enough, I gathered that much all by myself. I followed you here from Raif's. What'd he do?"

There's an edge of barely concealed anger in his words and I look up at him. I forget how protective he still is of me sometimes.

"It's fine, Luke. Promise. It'll be fine. He's just self-destructing, and I can't stand it." That's not quite a lie. I won't be responsible for dissention among the band. Raif needs his friends, regardless of what I might be feeling at the moment. "I took the day off special to help him with a song and he forgot. He was too drunk from last night and had to kick the latest girl out of his bed. It would have been smarter for me to go right back home. But you know me, I have to try and help." I sigh.

Luke's still rubbing my back, his cheek resting against my head as he holds me. "I'm sorry, Chloe. I've been considering giving him the come to Jesus talk, but wasn't sure we'd hit that point yet. I probably should have sat him down a week ago."

I reach up and pat his cheek. "It's not your fault. He's an adult behaving badly. We can't make him snap out of it. We just have to tolerate him while he works this out and hope we'll still want to be friends with him when he's done."

Luke chuckles. "Truer words were never spoken," he murmurs into my hair. He squeezes me tight. He's always made me feel loved, wanted. It's really a shame I could never make myself fall in love with him. He's a wonderful man and he's always been good to me. Even after I broke his heart in high school.

"Thank you for following me." I say, glad to have his comforting arms holding me.

"You know I'd do pretty much anything for you, love." He responds, his tone light, but I can feel the sincerity ringing in every word.

I turn in the circle of his arms, so I can see his eyes. "I don't deserve you." He shakes his head before I've finished the sentence.

"No, sweet tart. *You* deserve better. You deserve everything, but for some reason, you just don't see it. When are you gonna go looking for something good for yourself instead of looking out for everyone else?"

"I don't know," I tell him honestly. "I don't know if I know how."

"Well, if you ever want my help figuring it out, you let me

know." He drops a kiss on the top of my head and tucks me back into his embrace. And there we stay, sitting in companionable silence until the sun goes down.

The next day I go through the motions of my life. I go to work, I talk and joke with Zora and Lacey, the other Saloon waitress. I argue with Odetta about who the best female country singer ever is. Tammy Wynette according to her, Loretta Lynn in my opinion. I put on a decent show. Inside, I feel hollowed out. I've ignored more than a dozen calls from Raif. I'm sure his apologies are heartfelt and sincere, but I simply don't want to hear them. Not right now.

Luke was right about me. I've never sought out happiness for myself. I never thought that was even a possibility. But maybe it's time I start. And maybe the only way I can do that is to force myself to get over Raif Montgomery before he decimates my heart without even trying to.

I'm sequestered in the office around dinner time when there's a knock at the door and I know in my gut who's on the other side before he speaks.

"Chloe Jane? Can I come in, please?" I sigh and drop my head in my hands.

"Go away, Raif. I don't want to see you right now."

Of course, he ignores this and ducks inside the office instead. He closes the door behind him and leans against it, studying me. He looks haggard, his beard unkempt, his golden hair disheveled. His normally bright eyes are bloodshot with purple circles underneath. My traitorous heart weakens at the sight of him looking so downtrodden. I try and steel myself against it, but I fail.

"Damn it, Raif, I said *no*. Why am I having to repeat that word to you so much lately?" I ask waspishly.

He flinches like I hit him and my resolve to be cool to him crumbles. "I'm sorry, Chloe. I had to apologize. I know you're mad and you've every right to. I never should have been pawing at you like that, I never should have let you think for even a second that I'd throw our friendship away. Not for anything would I let you walk out of my life. You have to know that." He sounds desperate, talking so fast his words are tripping over each other to get out and be heard.

Frowning, I sit back in my chair and cross my arms protectively over my chest. I have to be tough on him right now. I have to stand up for myself or nothing in my life is ever going to get better. "No, Raif. I didn't know that. I can't read your mind, you know. I don't know what's been going on in your head these last few weeks."

He crosses to me in a few strides and leans over the desk, his hands braced on either side of the desk calendar, staring directly in my eyes. "Don't give up on me now, Chloe. Please?" He swallows, and I watch his throat work, watch as he fights to get himself under control. "I cannot lose you. I know I've been an ass and I've never deserved to have you in my life, but I'm begging you. Give me a chance to make this up to you."

I search his eyes and sigh, the last of my anger at him blowing away at the pain I see there. "Stop it," I say softly. "Just...don't. You don't have to make anything up to me, and I'm not saying you don't deserve my friendship. I just need you to think about your actions. You are my best friend, Raif." I get choked up, have to stop to send the dratted tears back down my throat. "If you ever kiss me again, it better not be because you're a mess. I'm not a backup plan. I'm not someone you can use and toss aside. I won't let you do that to me, no matter how I feel."

His sea colored eyes hook on mine, widening at my words. He

studies my face closely. "I promise you I *never* thought you were a backup plan, Chloe Jane. Never."

I nod at him. "Okay—" There's another knock on the office door and Raif's face falls. I swallow, glad for the reprieve from this fraught encounter. I said what I had to, now I'd be okay if Raif left so I could take a breath and get my heart out of my stomach. "Come on in." I say, grateful to whoever's on the other side of the door.

Luke's dark head pokes in, a smile on his face until he sees Raif and then storm clouds roll through his dark blue eyes. I smile wide at him and he returns it. "Hello, Luke. To what do I owe this pleasure?"

He holds up a Tupperware container and winks at me. Looks like he's going to ignore Raif's presence. "Hello, sweet tart. Mom made homemade strawberry shortcakes today and I thought of you."

I clap my hands excitedly. "Oh, yay. With her homemade whipped cream on them?" He grins at me, his eyes twinkling down at me.

"Yes, with her homemade whipped cream and the melt-in-your-mouth shortcakes that you love."

I grin at him as he offers the container to me. "You are my very favorite person right now, Luke Benson. Thank you." I tell him, and he chuckles.

"You are welcome." He drawls, his full lips tilted up. I get up and he grabs me in a tight hug. He kisses the top of my head and leans down to whisper in my ear, "I thought you could use a pick me up."

I smile up at him and say, "Thank you, Luke. Really."

"My pleasure." He kisses my cheek and steps back, and I see Raif leaning against the wall behind the door again. He's watching us, his eyes thoughtful.

Luke turns and finally acknowledges Raif. "Hello, brother."

Raif nods at Luke, no grin on his face. "Hello, yourself."

"Forgive me but you look like shit." Luke says. "You all right?"

Raif finally cracks a smile and says. "The whiskey ain't working anymore, I guess." Luke chuckles.

"It never really was. Just a bad look for you. Speaking of, I had an idea for a song, want to grab dinner and go talk about it?"

Raif nods. "That sounds good."

Luke squeezes me once more. "Can we bring you anything, sweet tart?"

I smile at them both, glad to see them joking around like usual. "Odetta might never forgive me if I let someone else feed me."

They both laugh and Raif comes over and folds me into his arms for a hug. I hug him back, my face pressed into his chest, listening to his heart beat. "Thank you," he murmurs into my hair, but I hear him. I step back and pretend to shoo them off.

"You boys go have fun." I tell them. "I have work to do."

Luke blows me a kiss and pushes Raif from the office. They're both smiling and when the door closes behind them, I am, too.

Raif

"TRY THAT A LITTLE FASTER," CHLOE URGES, HER VOICE excited. I grin at her and follow her instructions, strumming the notes at a faster pace. Chloe softly sings the lyrics we've been working on together for the last week and grins at me. "I think that's it." She says, bouncing with excitement.

I chuckle, nodding at her, "I think you're right. It was just too slow before." Chloe claps happily before downing the last of her lemonade. We're set up in my living room, the remnants of the fried-chicken-and-fixings dinner Odetta made for us littering the scarred surface of the coffee table my mom and I found at a secondhand shop.

It's been a few weeks since Chloe and I had our blowup. I've stopped moving through women the way I was. And I've cut back on my drinking. I feel happier now. Lighter than I've been in ages. Being sober more has given me time to think. I never realized how Pippa dragged me down, how she'd become more of a habit to me than someone I cared for. I used her as surely as she was using me. That's not the kind of man I ever thought I would be. These days my focus is on my music and the people I love. And I take things as they come. I'm trying to be the best man I know how to be. For me. And even though I know she deserves so much better than me, I want to be the man for Chloe. I know it makes me selfish, but now that I've tasted those lips, I know for sure. I'll never want anyone else.

"What're you thinking about so hard, cupcake?" Chloe's voice breaks in on my thoughts. "You look very serious all of a sudden."

I grin at her and shrug. "Just reflecting on how happy I am right now."

She smiles at me, bright and open as the sun and my breath catches in my chest for a moment. "Well, I'm glad to hear that."

I can hear the relief in her voice, the sincerity in that statement ringing in every syllable. Being with Chloe has always been easy, there aren't ever any games. I don't have to try and puzzle out hidden agendas in her actions or words. I can just be. She makes everything better. I open my mouth to tell her so and her cell phone trills an alert, startling us both. I close my mouth again. Timing isn't right. She checks the display on her phone and her face clouds over, the sunshine fading away at whatever she sees there.

"What's up?" Her lush mouth is turned down at the corners, her green eyes sad when she raises her face to meet my gaze. She gets to her feet, and I do the same, reaching for her instinctually, wanting to comfort her, bring her smile back. I can't stand the pain in her expression and experience tells me only one person has the power to put that look on her face. Lilly May must be up to her usual nonsense over at the saloon. I pull her into my arms. "Lilly May?"

"Yeah," she murmurs into my chest, her arms tight around my waist, her face hidden from me. I know she's embarrassed, even though her mother is an adult and Chloe can't control what she does. "I have to go deal with her. Zora says she's on something; barefoot and half dressed, loud and ranting. Must be great for business. I don't know why I'm surprised. It's the usual routine."

I tilt her chin up to look in her eyes and my heart hurts at the pain I see swimming in the green depths. "Can I come?" I know if I offer to help, she'll turn me down flat. She seems to think she has to do everything on her own. She tilts her head up at me, studying my eyes for a moment before answering.

"You wouldn't be trying to come to my rescue, would you, cupcake?"

Damn it, she knows me too well. "No. Honestly, I'm being selfish. If I come, too, I can get you back here after you're done. You haven't had a whole day off in weeks, Chloe Jane. If I don't go with you, you'll just stay to close up and I need you tonight. Clearly, we're very busy here." I grin down at her, wheedling for my way.

She returns my grin and I feel her body relax against mine. "So long as it's for purely selfish reasons. I don't need a white knight charging in to save me. I'm no damsel in distress."

"I'd never even think it." I tell her, trying to hold back a smile.

"Well then," she says, "I suppose if that's the case then you can come with me."

We make it to the Saloon in record time, Chloe's white-knuckled grip on the steering wheel the only outward sign of any stress she might be feeling. When we park out front, we see that Lilly May has been deposited outside of the saloon and is throwing a fit. Dressed in what looks to be a slip, barefoot, long hair wild around her face, she bellows and shrieks. A crowd of onlookers has gathered around to gawk at the spectacle. Chloe hisses out a soft curse, jumping out and leaving the engine running. I get out behind her, just in case. Her mother can be a tricky piece of work and I've seen her go on the attack physically before. Chloe won't defend herself, she hates violence, but I will not allow Lilly May Morris to do any more damage to her daughter if I can help it.

"I don't have to do what you tell me!" Lilly May shouts at Zora, her words coming out so fast they're hard to grasp. She's on her feet but looks unsteady, as Chloe and I approach the scene. Chloe's cheeks are pink as I glance at her and I hate that her mother does this to her still. Lilly May has been the talk of the town since we were kids. I know Chloe thinks people believe she's bound to take a turn and end up just like her mother, but I know better. Most people who know Chloe know she's the opposite of everything Lilly May is. Of course, there are a few old ladies who live to feel superior to everyone else, but who cares what they think? Someday, I hope Chloe can see the truth of the matter.

Zora sighs loudly, sounding exasperated. "You know you aren't allowed inside, Ms. Morris. I'm only enforcing the rules."

I watch Chloe square her shoulders and step into the fray, keeping her voice low and attempting to calm her mother down.

I turn to Zora, who looks half murderous, half sad and quietly ask, "Did you call the sheriff?"

Zora shakes her head at me wordlessly, her light brown eyes shimmering with sympathy for her boss. I step up next to Chloe while her mother wobbles closer to her, looking angry. I rest my hand on Chloe's shoulder supportively. Leaning down, I say into her ear, "Why don't we just bring her home? Eliminate the spectacle?" Chloe looks up at me, seeming surprised.

"You don't want to deal with her, Raif. You shouldn't have to—"

I cut her off, skimming my thumb down her cheek. "Neither should *you*. I can help. Let's get her home." Chloe's shoulders sag and she nods at me. I step forward and nudge Chloe back so I'm shielding her. Just in case. Lilly May is still screaming and carrying on. I hold my hands out in front of me in surrender and smile at Chloe's mother, suppressing the urge to throttle her.

"Lilly May Morris why are you out here causing a fuss?" I force my voice to sound playful and light. It's fake as hell, but she doesn't know that.

I watch as her blurry eyes search for me. She can't help herself. She always focuses on any male in her vicinity. Inwardly cringing, I watch understanding gather in her eyes as she looks me up and down again. I'll shower the feel of her undressing me with her eyes away later. Right now, I just want her out of the street so Chloe can relax again.

"Well, 'lo there, Raif. I didn't see you come over." She places one hand on her cocked-out hip and attempts to bat her eyelashes at me. I don't laugh at her, which I feel is commendable.

I keep a friendly smile on my face and offer her my hand. "Why don't you come with me and we'll get you back home where you belong?" I can feel the tension radiating from Chloe behind me, but I pretend that Lilly May is the only thing I see. Chloe's mother tilts her head at me, her eyes narrowing suspiciously.

"You're just doing *her* bidding." She finally whines, her eyes skating beyond me to her daughter. She steps closer, trying to get closer to Chloe but I stay between them. "She's just plain old selfish, trying to keep what's mine from me." Her voice is growing louder again, and I step closer, taking hold of her elbow.

"Hush now with that nonsense and let's go. You can come with us or we can wait for the sheriff. Again."

Her lower lip trembles as she watches my face carefully, trying to figure out if I'm serious or not. Finally settling on a pout, she mutters, "Fine." She flounces forward unsteadily, and I reach out and take her elbow to keep her on her feet. She not-so-graciously allows me to lead her to Chloe's truck where I deposit her inside, then follow her in.

Chloe climbs in the driver seat, her lush mouth set in a thin line, and faces forward, asking through her teeth, "Where are you living now?"

Lilly May presses herself against my side and I move closer to the passenger door in response. I don't want to give her any ideas. She whines and huffs at my silent rebuke and then turns to her daughter. "I'm staying with a friend. Over on Sycamore. You can just drop me at the corner. I don't want to put you out." Her voice is dripping with some false inflection I can't quite figure out, but I see Chloe's jaw tense and her hands go white-knuckled on the steering wheel.

"It's no more trouble than you showing up where you know you're not allowed on my only night off in three weeks was." Chloe snipes at her mother, her voice uncharacteristically hard. "Just give me the address." She sounds exasperated after mere minutes in her mother's presence and I can't really blame her. Lilly May was never much of a mother and there were far too many nights when Chloe climbed through my bedroom window, seeking solace and protection from whatever man her mother had brought home with her.

Lilly May pouts once more and rather than play into her mother's game, Chloe slams on the brakes, making us all jerk in our seats. She jerks the wheel, pulling over and putting the truck in park as she says, "Fine, don't tell me. You can get out right here and just go... *wherever*. But if you go back to the saloon, I'll make sure you spend tonight in a cell." She pauses and looks her mother in the eye, her eyes colder than I've ever seen them. "*At least* tonight." I watch Lilly May swallow and clench her own jaw and for a moment, I can see the resemblance between the two of them.

Chloe meets my eyes, nodding at me to let her mother out of the truck. I nod back and hop out, gesturing for Lilly May to follow. She looks murderously back at me before she scowls and starts swearing angrily at us both. "You are a spiteful, ungrateful little bitch." She snarls at Chloe as she scrambles out of the truck and stomps away barefoot, cussing the whole time.

I stand outside the truck, shocked, watching the angry woman depart until Chloe's voice sounds from inside. "Yep, that's me." She sighs. "C'mon cupcake, let's get out of here." She sounds exhausted, but when I turn to look at her, she's smiling wanly. All I want is to hold her and bring back the sunshine she was giving off earlier.

I climb back in the truck and grin at her. "Yes, lets."

Raif

The next night, the crowd at the Saloon is electric, their energy frenetic as we move through our set. The dance floor is full, the bar hopping, and the applause is off the charts as we finish a Garth Brooks medley. You can never go wrong with Garth. About ten minutes into our set, a dark-haired man I've never seen before came in and took a seat in front of Chloe at the bar. He stood out like a sore thumb in his very expensive looking suit. He has divided his attention between the band and Chloe ever since. I can't look away from them.

I'm mesmerized by the scene at the bar. Chloe's long brown hair is pulled back in a messy ponytail. She's wearing that damned denim mini skirt that hugs her rear end again. She's paired it with a short-sleeved blue flannel knotted above her belly button, leaving her midriff on display. The gleaming expanse of her bare tan legs flash as she moves behind the bar, her feet in simple black flip flops. She's drop-dead gorgeous and the suit at the bar seems to share my opinion because he's not moving.

I'm caught slightly by surprise when Luke leads us into our last song for the night, his fiddle flying through the intro. His dark hair falls into his eyes as he focuses all his energy on coaxing the melody out of the instrument. I break in with the vocals on one of our original songs and there is a female whoop from the crowd as one of our fans recognizes the tune. I haven't quite got used to the fact that there are people out there who know our songs by heart and come out to see us and sing along.

I look over and once again, Chloe is gracing the suit at the bar with one of her brightest smiles. Damn it, no. He's all wrong for her. I can just tell. I've been watching throughout our performance. I know better, I've felt Troy's and Luke's eyes on me a few times when I've been too engrossed in watching what Chloe's been doing instead of looking out over the crowd of people in front of the stage. But the guy in the nice suit who's been bending my girl's ear all night is stealing my good sense. I tell myself I'm just looking out for my best friend, but I don't believe it, and neither will the guys when they inevitably question me about my behavior later.

I belt out the last line of the song and Luke thanks the crowd for coming. The dark-haired man smiles at Chloe, who beams her brightest smile back at him and all sense flees my person. I make a beeline straight for Chloe, my eyes never leaving her. I come up next to her, behind the bar where only the employees are supposed to be and wrap my arm around her slim hips. I tug her into my body and can practically feel the confusion rolling off her in waves at my behavior.

"Hello there, Chloe Jane," I say, my voice deliberately intimate. "Who's your new friend?"

Chloe looks up at me, her green eyes wide and I smile at her as if she's the only person in the bar. She blinks at me and opens her mouth but before she can respond, the suit stands up, a strange grin on his face.

"It was great talking to you, Chloe," he says, dropping some bills on the bar. "I'll definitely be coming back again."

She reaches out a hand to him, sounding slightly panicked. "No, no. Wait one moment, I have something for you, Dell." Dell? She knows his name? She has something for him? My hand tightens on her hip and she elbows me sharply in the ribs. She glares up at me. "Behave yourself, Raif." There are two spots of color high on her cheeks, and I'm caught off guard all over again by how pretty she is, even out of sorts. "I'll be right back." She steps out of my reach and disappears into the office before I can respond.

The way-too-handsome stranger smirks at me and I glare harder at him. He's gotta be in his forties, there's no way he's right for Chloe. She just turned twenty-four in June. "You've got the wrong idea, cowboy." I feel my jaw clench tighter.

"Somehow I don't think so." I say through clenched teeth.

Chloe comes back out in time to hear my response and shoots me one of her death glares. She moves her laser eyes to the suit and hands him a cd.

"Here you go. Come back." She says, sounding so earnest I feel my chest ache at the loss of her. I hadn't even got up the nerve to tell her what I'd been thinking lately, and I've lost her.

"It was a pleasure to meet you, Chloe. This is a wonderful place you have." He grins at me and gives a little two finger salute wave thing and leaves. Luke and Bran meet us at the bar in time to see

Chloe glaring daggers up at me. She points wordlessly at the closed office door and I gulp.

"You two, too. And grab Troy, this concerns him as well." Chloe orders and Luke complies immediately.

"Yes, ma'am," he says, before wading into a sea of women currently vying for Troy's attention. I hear Luke mutter, "I need a damn whistle." Before Chloe tugs me into the office behind Bran.

I lean against the wall and watch her stand behind her desk, arms crossed over her chest staring me down. Bran is using a bandana from his back pocket to mop the sweat off his face, the room is dead silent. Luke ducks inside towing Troy in behind him a moment later. Troy's chambray shirt is half unbuttoned, his red hair a disaster. Clearly, he'd already chosen his bed buddy for the night. I'm kind of surprised Luke was able to pull him away.

Chloe waits until Troy closes the door behind him with a heavy sigh. "This better be important, Chlo, I was busy."

"You'll be busy again in five minutes, Troy. Don't start." Luke retorts before Chloe has the chance.

Planting her fists on her hips, Chloe turns her fury towards me. "What the hell were you thinking?"

"I was thinking he didn't leave your side through the whole set. He was clearly after something." I say, my face hot as I dig myself further into this hole I've started. Her face flames with what I think is anger.

"He was a record producer, Raif!" Chloe hisses at me. "He was talking to me about you guys!" She swallows and lifts her chin. "And even if he *was* after something else—that's *my* business."

Luke's eyes dance back and forth between us as Chloe stands there silently daring me to retort with anything but an apology for my boorish behavior.

"A record producer?" Bran clarifies into the tense silence, and Chloe nods.

"Yes. Dell Xander from Music City Records. He seemed impressed by you guys. I gave him your demo before he left."

Luke cuts a look at me. "What exactly transpired between you and the record producer that has sweet tart so pissed?"

Troy pipes up, "What the hell is a music producer from Nashville doing in White Oak?"

I look at Chloe's fiery eyes and swallow down a plea for forgiveness. I can do that later, after the boys have left. "I fucked up." I say simply. "I was worried he was messing with her, and I was rude."

"Of course you were." Luke mutters.

"Smooth." Troy mumbles as he pushes a hand through his unkempt hair.

"He was smiling when he left. Maybe it will be okay." Bran interjects before Chloe can savage me with the fury I see simmering in her face right now.

Troy cuts to the heart of the matter. "So, this guy came to listen to us and Raif got all alpha male asshole?"

"Excellent nutshelling." Luke chimes in unhelpfully.

"If he doesn't come back it's on me." I say, still holding Chloe's gaze.

"It'll be fine." Chloe says suddenly, her voice tired. "Just... it'll be fine." She straightens up, opens the top middle drawer on her desk and pulls out the saloon's checkbook. "Great job tonight, guys." Her tone is all business now. She writes out the check, detaches it and hands it to Luke. "There you are."

Luke scowls at her. We hate that she insists on paying us for playing here. She won't take any money for all the managerial stuff she does for us. "Have a good night, boys. I have some work to do." She continues, and I can tell from her tone she clearly means this as a dismissal of all of us. She's reached the limit on her patience and needs time to herself.

Luke looks daggers at me, but motions for Troy to open the office door. Bran looks around frowning, but Troy's already gone, so before he follows suit, he says, "Thanks for everything, Chloe."

Luke goes to her and puts a hand on her shoulder. "Can I do anything to help?" His voice is quiet and he's not looking at me anymore. I can feel something I can't name swelling from within him. Chloe looks up at him with such sadness in her eyes that it hurts to see it.

"No, I'm okay. Thank you. You get on home. I'll see you." She pats his arm comfortingly, her eyes killing me.

Luke nods and wraps her in a quick, fierce hug. "I'm just a call away if you change your mind." I feel the jealousy flare back to life inside me at his soft, sincere words. I don't like this. I don't get jealous, damn it. I definitely don't get angry at my friends over how well they treat Chloe. This is nuts, *I* am nuts.

Luke glares at me and nods towards the open door, "C'mon, Raif. I'll drive you home." That nameless emotion is back in his voice, in the set of his jaw, and I finally realize what it is. Laughing, affable, easy going Luke is pissed. At me if his glare is any indication. I open and close my mouth, unsure how to proceed.

Chloe meets my eyes, hers are full of confusion and I frown, feeling like a cad. "I'll walk it, brother. I'll see you tomorrow." Luke looks as though he'd like to argue with me, but he just nods and leaves after another long look at Chloe.

The silence in the room is thick with the weight of unspoken words once Luke leaves and I go to Chloe. I stand in front of her trying to find the right words to say to make this right. She looks up at me after a few long quiet moments pass between us.

"What is wrong with you?" she asks finally, her voice shaking.

I run my knuckles down her cheek and frown. "I'm sorry. I was an ass. I just...panicked." I tell her honestly.

Her eyes search mine, looking for truth maybe, or sanity, I'm not sure. But she eventually sighs. "Why are you panicking? Even if he was after something from me, Raif, we would still be friends. I don't understand."

I reach out and pull her into my arms, hugging her close, inhaling the sweet scent of her. She's rigid against me for a moment before her body goes pliant, relaxing against me. "I'm so sorry, I don't know what's wrong with me." I lie. I know what my problem is, I'm just too chicken-hearted to admit it to her. I can't lose her. "You're just important, Chloe. I know it's not right. You deserve better. I will do better. Okay?"

She looks up at me from within the circle of my arms and shakes her head. "Stop apologizing. Just don't do it again. You know I'm not going anywhere, Raif." She reaches up and lightly touches my jaw. She holds my eyes as she says with total sincerity, "No one is ever gonna take me out of your life."

I force a grin, cover her hand on my jaw with my own. "I know." But I don't. Not really. Heaven knows she deserves so much more than me, so much more than anything anyone in this podunk town can give her. But I'm selfish enough to hope that she will settle for me someday.

"Can you drive me home later?" I ask, threading our fingers together and then bringing hers to my lips.

"Of course," she murmurs, and I feel a shiver run through her. Hope springs to life inside me. Maybe I do have a shot.

Chloe

PULLING UP OUTSIDE OF RAIF'S HOUSE, I TURN TO HIM AND smile, hoping I don't look as tired and confused as I feel. Raif is tapping his feet against the floor, a nervous tick of his. I don't know what's up with him, but he's been acting strange since the rest of the band left the saloon earlier.

I don't want to kick him out of my truck, that would be mean. But all I want in the world right now is a hot bath and a cold beer. Preferably at the same time.

"I'll see you tomorrow?"

"Can you come in for a bit?" Raif asks at the same time.

"Sorry," I begin, but once again he speaks at the same time, this time saying the same thing I did.

I grin at him. "Jinx." That seems to break the tension that was brewing in him. His barely-there grin makes an appearance and I relax.

"C'mon inside with me and I'll give you a coke." His voice is low, his blue-green eyes glowing with some intent I can't pinpoint. I laugh, the childhood joke at odds with his low, husky voice in the small confines of the truck.

I open and close my mouth, considering my own motives as I watch his bright eyes twinkling at me. "I can come in, I suppose." He smiles at me like he just won the lottery and my heart thumps a little faster in my chest.

He's out and around to my side of the truck before I've unbuckled my seatbelt. I blink at him, surprised when he opens my door for me. He takes my hand and helps me down, threading our fingers together as we take the short walk to his front door. Once inside, he nudges me towards the sofa and smiles almost shyly at me, which is insane but still makes my breath catch in my chest.

"Sit. I'll get us a couple beers." His voice shakes a little and I flop down onto the sofa gracelessly. I have no idea what's going on here. I'm a little concerned Raif has lost his mind. Or he has something horrible to tell me? Disturbing possibilities start piling up in my mind while he moves to the stereo system and flips on the local country station. Kane Brown's voice fills the room and Raif joins me on the sofa. He twists the top off a bottle of Michelob and hands it to me.

"Thank you," I murmur, and then take a long pull from my bottle as he twists his own top off. I watch his throat work as he follows my lead, swallowing down half the bottle in one gulp. He's sitting so close that our knees are touching, and I can feel the heat of him through the worn denim of his jeans against my bare skin. Everything about him has all my senses on overload.

He sets his bottle down on a coaster on the coffee table in front of us and turns to me. I take another quick drink and set my own bottle down. He looks so nervous, it's making me nervous.

"Are you okay?" I ask. Clearly, he's working up to telling me something awful. I just have to make myself hear it. Maybe then I can help him through whatever it is.

He blushes and reaches out and tucks a stray lock of my hair behind my ear, making me shiver. "I—yeah. I just wanted to explain about earlier." He runs his knuckles over my jaw, grazes his thumb over my bottom lip and my pulse stutters.

I swallow, working to bring moisture into my mouth. "O-okay."

His eyes are hooked on my mouth, watching his thumb sweep over my lips and then slipping down to my chin. "I was jealous," he croaks out.

I want to ask him if he's suffered a stroke or some other neurological event, but I don't think he'd take that well. If he keeps touching me, though, I'm going to melt into a puddle on his couch. "Raif—" I manage and then his thumb is stroking a feather light path up my throat, his fingers cupping the back of my neck, and I forget how to talk.

"I've been so close to telling you so many times the last few weeks." His voice is soft, his eyes on mine now.

I blink at him. My brain is numb. I don't understand. Jealous? Why is he jealous? What has he wanted to tell me?

"Tell me what?" My heart is thudding out of control, and I think I might be on fire. It's so hot in here suddenly.

"I want you so bad," he says softly. My brain short circuits, my body freezing in shock as he moves closer and settles his mouth over mine. Fireworks explode in the pit of my stomach as his hand moves into my hair, tilting my head back so he can deepen the kiss. Raif slips his tongue between my lips, sliding it against mine and jump-starting my body into action.

71

My hands move from their limp flop in my lap. One finds its way into Raif's silky blonde hair. The other fists in the front of his t-shirt, hanging on to him like he might disappear if I let go. I know I should stop him. I should stop kissing him back. I should definitely stop the needy breathless sounds that keep escaping from within me. But I can't. I've wanted this closeness with him for too long. Knowing he wants me too is heady. Even after I told him he'd better be sure if he ever kissed me again, he's kissing me. I can't deny either of us this experience. Even if it's only for a night, I'll take the heartbreak that could follow if I get to share this with him.

Raif kisses me like he'll die if he stops. His tongue dances masterfully with mine, exploring my mouth and making me dizzy with want. I give up on sanity and just let myself get swept away in the sensations he's bringing to life in me. His mouth breaks from mine and I whimper, wanting his lips back on mine. His eyes blaze down at me, blue-green fire and he groans, trailing scorching kisses along my jaw. My head lists to the side automatically granting him access to whatever part of my body he's interested in. His mouth finds its way to my neck, nipping and sucking and my hands tighten on him in response, my body trembling with need. Eager lips seek out my ear, his teeth closing gently on the lobe and I gasp, arching into him.

"Is this okay?" Raif rasps into my ear, his breath hot against my skin. "I don't want to go too fast for you. I want you to be sure about us."

All my feeble worries disappear with his words. This is Raif and I know there's not a dishonorable bone in his body. No matter what, we'll get through whatever results from this bout of possible insanity. I hold his eyes as he waits patiently for me to respond. Leaning in, I do what I've longed to a million times over the course of our friendship. I kiss him softly. He follows my mouth as I pull away, trying to stay in the kiss longer. Reveling in the fantasy that's coming to life right now, I move my fingers lightly over his face.

"I'm sure, Raif." I trace his cheekbones, the slight arch of his eyebrows, his jaw, my fingers shaking. The feel of the scruff of his beard under my touch makes me smile as I whisper, still holding his gaze. "I want you, too."

Raif's answering smile is incandescent. In a heartbeat, his mouth is back on mine, both of his hands in my hair. This kiss is almost feverish, his mouth hungry on mine, his fingers moving deftly in my long hair as he works it out of its ponytail. My mouth is open under his, my hands clutching at his shoulders as my head spins from his kisses. Suddenly, Raif pulls his mouth from mine, dropping hot kisses on my neck before he stands. He moves so fast, I almost fall off the couch, my body was leaning so heavily into his. He pulls me to my feet and then scoops me into his arms before I even have a chance to protest the motion. He carries me into his bedroom, laying me down gently on top of the quilt.

"I've wanted you here with me forever." His eyes move over me and I feel it like a physical caress even though I'm still fully clothed. I reach for him, unwilling to wait to touch him now that this is happening.

"I'm here now." I tell him, as he kneels on the bed. "Come here," I demand, and lean up to meet him halfway as he hovers over me.

"Yes ma'am," he drawls before claiming my mouth with a searing kiss. For a few glorious, hot moments, all I can do is feel as our hands explore each other's bodies for the first time. Our mouths fuse together for long moments, sharing breath. Our hands are eager, any trace of hesitance gone. I pull his tee shirt over his head and toss it behind him. He's perfect, his muscles defined but not overtly so, and I run my hands over his naked torso, learning the texture of his warm skin. Raif holds himself still as I trace ridges of muscles, letting me explore. When my hands reach his stomach, he groans, and I freeze. I'm shocked that my touch could elicit such a response.

"You're beautiful," I tell him sincerely, looking in his eyes. He flushes and shakes his head at me. He leans in, kissing me sweetly.

"I'm nothing special compared to you, Chloe," he says against my mouth.

Frowning, I shiver and kiss him again. "I think you know I don't believe that's true." I lean up slightly, so our foreheads are touching. "I think you are perfect."

He kisses me like I'm all that's real in the world. His hands tangle in my hair as he presses me back against the bed, letting his weight settle on me. I wrap my arms around his trunk and hang on tight to him. His fingers sift through the length of my hair, following strands down my chest as he kisses me breathless. His hand rests next to my head to hold him up, the other begins exploring my chest over my worn flannel shirt. He unties the knot at my waist and begins unbuttoning the shirt from the bottom, his fingers skimming underneath against my bare skin after each button comes undone. He's setting me on fire a few inches at a time.

When he's unfastened all the buttons, he pulls back just a little, straddling my hips and peeling the sides of the shirt apart like he's unwrapping a gift. His gaze is reverential as his eyes move over my simple black lace bra. His hand settles warm and large on my stomach and I pull my bottom lip between my teeth to stop a moan from escaping. He slides his hand up, cupping my breasts through my bra, making my breath come faster. He's watching my face when he unclasps the front closure and slides his hands under both loosened cups. He fills his hands with my breasts, testing their weight, playing with my nipples until they're tight and straining for even more attention from him. His eyes never leave mine.

My lip stays clamped between my teeth until he leans down, his hands still fondling my chest. He nips playfully at my lower lip. "Does this feel good, Chloe Jane? When I touch you like this?" His voice is like velvet against my overstimulated senses.

My face flushes at the question but I hold his eyes as I admit, "Yes."

He grins that barely- there grin that melts my heart. He kisses me, more demanding now as he peels the bra down my shoulders. Raif breaks the kiss to say, "Sit up for me."

I do as he bids me, sitting up, feeling dazed and exposed as he slides the shirt and then the bra from my arms and lets them both fall to the floor next to the bed. I'm naked from the waist up now and I can feel his eyes seemingly memorizing every detail of the flesh on display. He presses me back down, his hands everywhere as his mouth claims mine. I run my hands over his naked back, down to his hips and then back up again. I hook one of my legs around his hip to keep him flush against me.

His fingers are playing at the waist of my denim skirt, then his hand skirts the top of my panties and my brain kicks in for half a second to wonder what condition those panties are in. Hopefully they're respectable because I blink and he's pulling my skirt off my hips. I look down and see I'm wearing the black lace bikini panties that match the simple bra. Oh good. Nothing embarrassing then.

Raif pulls my skirt all the way off my legs and lets it slip from his fingers as he sits back on his haunches at the foot of the bed. His blue-green gaze is moving up and over my body and he looks almost awed at what he's seeing.

"I never thought I'd ever be this lucky." He murmurs, climbing back up the bed and situating himself with one leg between mine and one on the other side. His hands are on my thighs, moving up over my hips and he drops a hot wet kiss on my inner thigh. I squirm restlessly. His hands travel north over my panties, up to my ribs and over my breasts. He sighs, his touch slow and deliberate. "Your skin is like silk."

I swallow hard, my breathing going wonky at his words, his touch, and the husky sincerity I hear in his voice. "Raif..." I begin but I don't know what to say and become overwhelmed by the emotions swirling inside me.

He looks down at me and smiles, like he understands. "If you change your mind at any time, you just say stop. Promise me."

"I don't want to stop. I won't want to stop." I feel like I've never spoken a truer sentence in my life.

Raif meets my eyes and braces himself above me again, lowering his mouth to my stomach while holding my gaze. My breath catches while he kisses a hot path up my body, pausing for a long moment at my breasts. His mouth closes around my flesh, his teeth grazing my nipple, and I feel the pleasure everywhere. He treats my other breast to the same treatment and I whimper, squirming beneath him. My hands pull at his hair as I go liquid and hot at once. I tug him up to kiss my mouth as my hands wander over his body.

We kiss with abandon, our bodies pressing closer together. I reach between us to work at his heavy leather belt. I want it off, all of it. I want him naked and pressed against me. I want him inside me. I want him shaking and calling out my name. And I don't think I have ever wanted anything this bad before.

I get his belt unbuckled, unzip his jeans and then my hand is inside. I run my fingers over the hot, hard length of him over the boxer briefs he wears. He groans out my name and freezes with his hand on my hip. He bites at my neck when I slip my hand inside his underwear, finally finding his bare skin with my own. He pushes into my hand, throbbing for me. I moan softly, and he breathes harder against my neck.

"I want you now," I admit, still stroking him.

He groans again and pulls his face out of my neck to look in my eyes. His hand slips inside my panties and the room goes hazy around me when his fingers slide against my center. He's grinning now as he touches me slow and torturous. I hold his eyes as I keep stroking him despite the pleasure he's building inside me. His thumb slips over my nub and I moan. His mouth comes down on mine again, biting at my lips, seeking to devour me. I move my hand out of his pants to get them off.

He moves his hips back out of my reach, so I can't maneuver his jeans off his hips and I growl at him. He chuckles at me, the sound doing nothing to tamp down the need zinging through me. One of his thick fingers slips inside me as he whispers right in my ear, "My pants aren't coming off until I'm *sure* you're ready for me, Chloe Jane."

I groan, gasping out a, "Please—" as a second finger slips inside me, his thumb still making me crazy from the outside. His fingers thrust deeper. Is he kidding? I don't think I can get any readier for him at this point.

He moans when I beg, drops down to bring one of my nipples into the wet heat of his mouth. My hips move with his ministrations, my hands fisted in the quilt beneath me. And then I break, my body shattering into bliss. The world goes fuzzy as I lay there panting and shaking with the aftershocks.

Raif claims my mouth in a searing kiss, his hand still in my panties, his fingers still inside me. He says against my mouth, "*That* was beautiful. Thank you."

I blush and smile at him. "I'll have a sassy reply for you once my brain starts working again."

He grins and kisses me again, removing his fingers from inside me. He slides my panties down, following their descent until he pulls them off my ankles. I sit up, following him, reaching for his jeans to get them off, too, and he lets me push him onto his back on the bed. I tug his jeans and boxer briefs off and then straddle his hips, leaning down to kiss his mouth. While I'm distracted by his mouth, I feel him reaching for something. I pull back and see he has a foil packet in his hand. I'm glad one of us is thinking at least.

He surprises me, turning the tables, rolling us over until I'm on my back again, with him above me. He sits back from me a moment and I watch him as he rolls the condom on. I blink and he's kissing me again. He presses me back against the bed and follows me down, his weight pleasant on me. Raif hooks my knee around his hip, his hand under my thigh supporting it as he enters me. We both moan as he fills me perfectly, both soothing the ache that's been building and making it worse. He rests a moment, his hips still, his forehead pressed to mine as we share breath, panting into each other's open mouths. We're staring into each other's eyes, adjusting to this new development between us, so many things being said without a word being spoken aloud.

Like some internal alarm sounds, our mouths fuse together once again as his hips finally move. A timeless dance begins between our bodies, the night dissolving around us in heat and pleasure.

I wake up a little at a time. I'm so comfortable, I don't want to move a muscle. I'm warm, but I don't feel my familiar comforter wrapped around me. And I had the most deliciously naughty dreams. I don't want them to end. I stretch and feel my body rejoice, sliding against a warm, very male form. I open my eyes and find the golden hair of my best friend on the pillow next to me. Not a dream then.

He's still asleep so I can study him unchecked. He looks peaceful and beautiful in sleep. All around me I can smell us – sex, sweat, my shampoo, his cologne. It's a heady combination. Raif has me cradled against his chest while he sleeps like I'm a live teddy bear. I don't mind. I reflect on all the carefully drawn lines we hopscotched over last night, more than once. But rather than the fear I was sure would overwhelm me, there's a sense of rightness. A peace inside me. Maybe it's physical satisfaction? I don't know, but I like it.

I reach over and run my fingers through Raif's hair, pushing it off his face. He smiles in his sleep and murmurs my name and my heart swells to twice its normal size. I press a soft kiss to his lips and he returns it without opening his eyes. I smile against his mouth and he kisses me again.

"Mornin', Chloe Jane," he says, then yawns hugely. "I could get used to waking up like this, smelling you on my sheets and your hair tickling my nose."

I giggle and then we both hear it, someone's letting themselves in the front door. My first horrified thought is it's Pippa, but then I remember that I had the locks changed after she left Raif at the altar. Then Luke's voice bellows from the other room.

"Get your ass out of bed, Montgomery," he calls, but not in his usual jovial tone.

I freeze, staring wordlessly at Raif. He pulls the quilt up and covers me, then slips out of bed, grabbing his jeans off the floor and pulling them on. He zips them but leaves them unbuttoned. "I'm up," he calls back to Luke. "You could've called. Or knocked." There's something wrong with his voice, too. He holds up a finger to me, whispers, "Don't move. I'll get rid of him."

I shake my head to disagree with this plan, but he's already gone. I'm alone wrapped in the quilt that smells of the night we shared. Why would he not want Luke to know? I mean, sure it's not anyone's business but ours, but the boys are all like brothers. It's bound to come out that Raif and I are more than friends now. Unless he doesn't want to be more than friends after all? Could I have been wrong about his intentions? I know Raif wouldn't try to hurt me. But he doesn't know I've been in love with him most of my life. He was looking for pleasure from someone he could trust, and I'd built this whole different kind of scenario in my head.

I wrap the quilt closer around me and creep out of the bed, moving to the bedroom door. I need to get out of here. I don't want to hear anything they might be saying out there. I have to get to work anyhow. I close the door and dress quickly, humming quietly to myself so I can't make out the boys' exchange. I scrape my long hair into a messy ponytail, sure it's a disaster but past caring. The need to get away is pounding through my veins, making me dizzy. Once I'm sure I'm all buttoned and as put together as I'm gonna get, I open the door and try and force my face into normal lines. With any luck, I can make an unnoticed exit.

Unfortunately, that's not to be. I take one step into the hallway and come face to face with a very unhappy looking Luke. I plaster a smile on my face, trying to ignore the tension simmering between the guys. Luke smiles like he has a toothache and says, "Oh. G'morning, Chloe." I can't remember the last time he called me by my actual name, but I move through it, not letting myself stop.

"Hi Luke. I was just leaving." I turn to see Raif looking unhappy in the small kitchen.

"I was gonna cook you breakfast," he says, hurt all over his handsome face.

"I'm sorry, cupcake. I have to get to work. Zora's off today." I shoot them both a too big smile and I wave. "I'll call you later. You boys have a good day."

And then I flee.

Raif

Luke and I watch Chloe practically run out of the house. He looks murderous. I don't know what to think about her running out like that. Most likely she came to her senses and took off. I try to tamp down the panic at that thought as Luke takes a menacing step towards me.

"What in hell do you think you're doing with her, Raif?" For the first time in all the time I've known him, there isn't an ounce of friendliness anywhere in his voice or face.

I stand my ground and glare back at him. "I don't know why you're upset about this, Luke. It's not your business. You know *me*, you know I'm never gonna hurt her!"

"I don't know anything about you right now. You're two months on the other side of a wedding that didn't happen to a demon bitch from hell. Three weeks from whoring your way through town." He steps closer. "I don't want you rebounding Chloe, because she'll do anything for you, Raif. And you're lonely and sad, and you're not trustworthy right now."

My hands clench into fists and I set my jaw, trying to bury the hurt feelings that his words bring. A voice in my head laughs at me. Other than Chloe, this is my closest friend telling me I'm a piece of shit who's bound to hurt the girl I love more than any other. Is this what everyone will think? I unclench my jaw, shake out my fists and look up at the man I've considered a brother for most of my life.

"I love her, Luke. I won't hurt her. I know I don't deserve her. You didn't have to tell me that. Hell, no one has to tell me that." Folding my arms across my chest, I stare him down. "Do you really think that little of me?"

Luke still looks pissed as hell, but his shoulders seem to relax. "I'm not saying you'd do it on purpose, Raif. But Chloe has a giant soft spot for you, and I think you might be the only person who doesn't know it. I don't want her hurt. You're not steady right now. I'm not trying to hurt you, but I care about her. I won't stand by silently and let you break her heart. She doesn't deserve that."

I open and close my mouth. There isn't anything left to say really. I know he's trying to protect Chloe. I'm starting to see that there's a reason Luke doesn't date. Luke's in love with Chloe, too. *Fuck.*

"I know you're looking out for her, brother. I can't fault you for that. I can promise you that I will *let* you break my nose if I hurt her. It's the very last thing I ever want to do."

"Fuck me, I hate your stupid ass," Luke hisses at me, but I note there's a decided lack of venom to his tone now. He sounds more like himself. I relax slightly. I never thought he and I would ever have to compete for the same girl. I never thought I'd let myself try for anything with Chloe. I thought she was far out of my reach.

"I hate you, too." I tell him with a grim smile. He nods in response then flops down on my couch. Where everything started with Chloe last night. I sigh. This morning was not supposed to go down this way. She was supposed to stay, we were supposed to talk, maybe spend the day in bed, getting better acquainted with each other's bodies.

"Well, now that we got that out of the way," Luke deadpans, cutting into my thoughts of Chloe, naked and shaking beneath me in my bed. Luke drops his head into his hands, elbows resting on his knees.

"Want some coffee?" I ask.

He grunts at me and I take that as a yes.

Last night I made the decision to man up and admit my feelings to Chloe. And I failed. I got caught up in how badly I wanted her. *Because you're a total fuckup,* my head provides. The result is she knows I wanted sex, not that I'm in love with her. She doesn't know that I want a future, the whole deal—with her. I have to tell her everything today. No matter how scared I am about her laughing in my face as a response.

I park my old Jeep outside of the saloon around twelve-thirty. It's time to publicly stake my claim to the best person I know, the only girl I want. Inside, Hank Warner is at the counter, like he always is at this time of day. Lacey is taking an order at a table by the empty stage. Chloe is behind the bar, her head buried in her laptop, a scowl marring her pretty face. Her long dark hair is down, falling like gleaming mahogany down her back and over her shoulders. I love when she wears her hair down, but she hardly ever does when she's at work. She says it gets in the way.

She's dressed in a pair of holey jeans that are so tight they look painted on and a black V-neck t-shirt with an open purple flannel button down over it. She looks damn good. She always looks good, this isn't surprising. Maybe it's because I've seen her naked now, touched and tasted her body, watched her fall apart, but all I can think about is having her that way again. As soon as possible.

I walk around to the employee side of the bar nodding to Hank as I pass. I stop right beside Chloe whose face flushes, but she doesn't look up from what she's working on. I swallow, working up my courage. It's now or never. Her chest rises with a swift inhale and then she raises wary green eyes to mine. I lean down and kiss her full on the mouth, taking my time and letting everything I feel for her flow through the kiss. At first, she's frozen, her mouth in a tense line under mine. But after a moment, she melts against me, kissing me back. She leans into me, one of her hands grabbing hold of my shoulder.

Lacey whistles in the background, Hank chuckles and Odetta mutters, "Well it's about damn time." Chloe tenses up again when she hears Odetta's voice, and I pull back, resting my forehead against hers.

"You left me."

She looks up at me, wide-eyed and gnaws on her bottom lip. "I had to come to work." But I can see there's more going on behind her eyes.

Odetta steps out from the kitchen and tuts at us both. "Why don't you two take this show into the office. You're gonna give Hank here a coronary if you keep it up."

"Hush, woman. My cable's out. This is the most entertainment I've had in days." Hank retorts and Chloe blushes hotter.

I brush my knuckles over Chloe's jaw and down her neck. She shivers and holds my eyes.

"Can I talk to you in the office?" I ask her softly.

She nods and allows me to tangle our fingers together to go into the office saying to Odetta, "Just knock if you need me."

Odetta shoots her an amused look, and pointedly glances around the near empty saloon. "Chloe, honey, I'm pretty sure I can handle anything that comes wandering in. Take your time."

Chloe grimaces and allows me to lead her into the office. I close the door behind me and lean against it, tugging on Chloe's hand until she's standing right in front of me. I widen my stance and put my hands on her hips, bringing her right up against me. Her pulse is thundering away in her neck. I wrap my arms all the way around her, linking my hands together at the small of her back.

Chloe rests her hands on my chest and looks up at me, her wide green eyes taking me in, a question lurking there. There's so much uncertainty mixed in with the heat simmering in her gaze. I lean down and claim her mouth with mine once again. I let my hands wander down to her rear end and keep her up against me that way. She gasps into my mouth and presses closer against me, kissing me back. I pull my mouth away to drop kisses along her jaw to her neck, where I find I left a mark on her last night. I nip the spot, unbelievably turned on by the sight, and she groans softly. I kiss the bruise and suck lightly.

"Sorry darlin', I didn't mean to leave a mark." I tell her, but I'm rock hard and ready to have her again just from seeing this small, accidental claiming. I press my hips into hers, so she can feel what she does to me and she lets out a quick exhale.

"I had to leave my hair down to cover it." She murmurs, her voice soft.

I nip at her earlobe, kiss back over her jaw to her mouth. "Well, I'll do it all the time, then, to see you with your hair down."

Her eyes swing back to mine, wider than ever. "You think so, cupcake?" I notice the quirk to her lips, the laugh hiding in her voice.

"Oh yeah." I kiss her again. "Do you disagree?"

"I think I do."

I grin down at her, sobering when I see the uncertainty still present in her green eyes. "Let's talk about why you left this morning."

"What's going on with you and Luke?" she counters, her hands still resting lightly on my chest.

I wrap a lock of her hair around one of my fingers, enjoying the silky feel, trying to order my thoughts into a coherent response without confessing things that aren't mine to tell. "He could tell I was off last night. He was worried I'd done something to upset you again." It's a slightly altered version of the truth. I wouldn't lie, I just can't tell her his motivation came from his own feelings for her.

She frowns up at me. "I don't want to be causing trouble between you guys."

I shake my head, continue working my fingers through her hair. "No, you aren't. We're okay. I promise you."

She holds my eyes then finally nods. "Okay." She stretches up and kisses my mouth again, her arms coming up around my neck to play in my hair and I lose myself in her for a few glorious moments.

When we break apart, we're both breathing heavy. I gather my control over my body and gently push her back. "We need to talk," I say, my voice gravelly with lust. "There are things I need to say, things I know you need to hear. Reassurances I need to make."

Chloe smiles at me. "Right now, all I need is for you to kiss me, Raif."

Raif

I knock on Chloe's kitchen doors that night at nine pm sharp. She promised to let Odetta close the saloon, so we can talk. She slides the door open wearing black leggings and an oversized gray tank top, her dark brown hair pulled back in a messy bun. She's never looked sexier. I grin at her and offer up my token, a sunflower I picked from one of the flower beds in the town square on my walk over here.

She smiles, her cheeks flushed, her big green eyes sparkling at me. "Thank you."

"You're welcome, darlin'." I stay on the threshold, waiting to be invited in, wanting to get this right. After everything, I can't mess things up now.

She steps back, one dark eyebrow quirked at me. "You coming inside, cupcake? Or are you waiting on an official invitation?"

"I wanted to do it right," I tell her, feeling my cheeks flush with embarrassment.

Her face softens, and she steps forward grabbing my hand and tugging me inside. "Get in here, please. We have things to discuss."

The apartment is small, just a few rooms above the bar. It used to be storage. It's got a small kitchenette with a café table and chairs that look out towards the patio through the sliding glass doors. A small living room with a beat up old overstuffed sofa and a small television. A stereo, of course. And one lone hallway off the entry from downstairs that leads to a tiny little bathroom and a small bedroom. The walls are covered with framed photos; the band, Chloe with me, with Daisy, with Luke, her grandparents. It feels cozy here.

I follow her in and pull her into my arms. Right here is where she belongs. I hug her close, inhaling her sweet, sunshine scent. "Yes, we do."

She lets me hold her as long as I want which is something I've always loved about Chloe. She's never in a hurry for me to let her go. She rubs my back, and I lean down, and she meets me halfway for a kiss. When she pulls back, I follow her mouth and she grins. "Come on. Let's have a seat." She leads me to the couch where we sit side by side. But instead of turning the tv on, like we normally would, she turns sideways and folds her legs under her, so she can look at me.

I mimic her and reach over to take her hand in mine. She smiles at me, watching our fingers tangle together, her thumb running over mine. It's nice, being with her like this. It's easy as breathing, feels natural even. "What are you thinking?" I ask her, my heart in my throat.

"I'm thinking you said you wanted to talk." She counters with her bottom lip back between her teeth.

I swallow hard and decide I have to be the brave one. Now that the time has come, I'm scared. I know if I want to be happy, though, then I have to take the leap. And hopefully, if I do, then Chloe will join me. "This is flat out terrifying," I tell her. Her fingers tighten around mine. "I hope you know, this isn't just about sex." I lick my lips, holding her eyes with mine. "Not for me, anyway. I think I've been at least half in love with you since the day I met you, Chloe Jane."

Her green eyes go wide and a single tear drips down her cheek. "Is that so?" she asks quietly, her lips quivering.

I nod, tightening my hold on her hand. "Yeah, it's true. I used to think it was just because you were a girl and I was protective because of your mom." I squeeze her hand when she flinches at the mention of her mother and our shared past. "But then I met Pippa and what I felt for her was so different than what I feel for you." I feel her hand tense within mine and rush to go on, before she gets the wrong idea. "Pippa was always more of a punishment I inflicted on myself." I admit. Still ashamed that I wasn't as good a man as I'd thought. "She was what I thought I deserved."

Chloe's watching my face steadily as she listens. "You've never seen yourself as you truly are, Raif." she murmurs softly. "You deserve much more than the way she treated you all those years."

I shake my head, "I don't know about all that, darlin'. I only know that I knew you were special. You were way too good for the likes of me. For the likes of anyone in this town. You belonged in some kind of fairy tale story with princes and a fairy godmother. That's what I always wished for you. A happily ever after to make up for all the darkness you had to live through."

I watch her face as she takes it all in. "Raif, I never wanted a fairytale."

I refrain from pointing out that she's never seemed to want anything for herself. Chloe's always looking out for me, for the band, for her grandfather before his death. But she never thinks about herself and what she wants and that makes me sad. "I know you didn't. I know you."

"I know you do."

I look in her eyes, see the fear mingled with the affection I know she feels for me. I know Chloe. I know she wouldn't just fall into bed with me unless she had feelings, too. The more than friendship kind of feelings. I swallow, decide it's now or never. "I've been doing a lot of thinking lately, a lot of soul searching. And I think you need to know..." I take a deep breath. "I'm sorry, but I'm in love with you, Chloe Jane. I don't want anyone else, just you. *Us.* That's what I want. Can we do that?"

She smiles tremulously. "You love me." It's not a question but I nod. She doesn't look surprised so much as triumphant. Like she's just had something proven to her. I watch her face, waiting for whatever might come next. "You really love me?" she asks, her voice shaking, her lips trembling.

I reach for her, pull her closer to me, wanting, no *needing* to hold her. "Yes, I do. I love you, Chloe Jane Morris. I think I always have and I just didn't know what it was."

She crawls closer to me, climbing into my lap. Tears are streaking down her cheeks, unchecked. Her smile could light up the whole town in a blackout. "I love you, Raif Montgomery," she says, and the tension leaves my body. *Finally.* I don't know how long I've been longing to hear those words from her, but it feels like an age. Her mouth is mere inches from mine as she murmurs, "I've loved you forever. I don't know how to stop."

I pull her even closer. "Don't ever stop, darlin'." I plead with her as she moves forward and sears my mouth with her kiss.

She pulls back after a moment and breathlessly says against my mouth, "We should make some rules. No lies." She kisses me again. "I mean it, Raif— total, brutal honesty."

I kiss her again and then break off to add the most important rule for both of us. "No running, Chloe Jane."

She holds my gaze with her own for several frantic beats of my heart and then I see her swallow. She nods. Her voice is shaky when she agrees. "No running."

With her words, it's as if something moves inside me, unleashing a flood of emotion; lust, love, and need all clawing through me, burning to be released. I settle my hands on her hips, shifting her so she's straddling me. I take her face in my hands, hoping to convey without any further clumsy words how precious she is to me. I bring her mouth to mine again, one hand moving into her hair, my fingers tunneling gently through until I've worked the elastic band out of the heavy silken tresses. I toss the elastic over my shoulder and sift her hair through my hands, using it to tilt her head how I want it as we kiss.

I break the kiss to nibble at the delectable bend of her neck and her head falls back, granting me access to explore the area more thoroughly. I keep one hand on her lower back to keep her against me and she squirms deliciously, making us both moan at the friction she's creating. I take my time kissing and sucking over the sensitive skin of her neck to her jaw and then down her throat.

"Raif..." Chloe's voice is breathless and cuts off on a groan when my mouth reaches her chest. With my teeth, I tug at the neckline of her tank top until the tops of her breasts come into view. Those luscious curves are encased in tight teal lace. It might be the sexiest thing I've ever seen. I pause to take in the sight of her and her face flushes, her eyes skirting away from mine. I cup one of her breasts over the soft material of her tank top and she arches into my touch, her pulse jumping in her throat. I pull the shirt over her head, dying to see the rest of her.

"You're so gorgeous, Chloe." I say before she's kissing me again, her hands on my jaw and my neck, keeping me close. My hands are on her chest, teasing her breasts through the cups of her bra. I break off the kiss, sliding my tongue under the lace confining her heavy breasts. She grinds against me and I growl when her hands slide up my bare chest. I somehow missed her removing my tee shirt, but I tune back in as her hands make their way to my belt. Her fingers are shaky as she gets past my heavy buckle and onto the button fly of my old jeans.

She whines, and I smirk at her. "Something the matter, darlin'?"

"Why can't you ever wear sweatpants?" She asks as she undoes the buttons with fingers that are clumsy with passion.

I chuckle but then her hand is slipping inside my jeans. My chuckle turns to a groan when she finds what she's seeking. I'm throbbing for her inside my boxer briefs. I expel a quick breath when her deft fingers close around my shaft moments later. I groan out her name. She smiles naughtily at me before kissing me breathless.

Holding myself still to allow Chloe to explore me to her heart's content is not easy. She seems to be trying to memorize the feel of my length under her touch. My heart is pounding out of control, my breath coming in desperate pants when she breaks our kiss and moves off my lap. I frown, following her but she pushes me back onto the couch and tugs my pants and boxer briefs off and then settles herself on her knees between mine.

Everything feels foggy around me. Just the sight of her on her knees between my legs is making it hard to breathe. Then both of her hands are between my legs, stroking and squeezing, teasing me until I am moving into her touch, craving more. She smiles saucily up at me and then leans down, taking my length in her mouth.

"Chlo—" My head falls back against the sofa as she closes her mouth around my girth and sucks lightly. "You don't have to." I manage around a moan of pleasure.

She doesn't stop, just keeps up what she's doing, tasting me, swirling her tongue around my tip. I thread my fingers through her hair and she sucks a little harder, moves her mouth up and down over my shaft. My intent wasn't to guide her motions, but it feels so good, I can't help tugging harder on her hair. I move my hand to the back of her neck to keep her where she is, with my length hitting the back of her throat. My hips long to move, but I keep still, only my fingers pulling on her hair. I think about anything but the way she looks right now; half naked in teal lace on her knees with me in her mouth. I let go of her neck and her head bobs up and down, the wet heat of her mouth encasing me, bringing me closer to climax.

This was not the plan. The plan was to take my time and worship her body. I wanted to make her beg for me, bring her more pleasure than she'd ever felt before. Instead, she's unraveling every ounce of control I've learned since I was a teenager. The evening's going to be over before long if she keeps it up.

"Chloe," I try again as she takes me deeper. "Hang on." I plead, and she does so immediately. She pulls back and lets me slip from her mouth.

I take her in, her cheeks are flushed, her lips swollen, her hair disheveled. "God you're sexy." I tell her, and she blushes hotter and leans up to claim my lips in a kiss. I pull her up so she's on my lap again, sitting sideways now, her legs hanging between mine.

She bites my earlobe and asks, "Do you not like that?"

I groan and pull her mouth back to mine, kissing her with everything I'm feeling. When I break away, I speak against her mouth. "No, darlin', it's not that. I liked it a little too much. I didn't want to end the party too soon."

She flushes darker and I groan, so turned on I can hardly stand it. "We wouldn't want that," she agrees, her luminescent green eyes hooked on mine. I run my hands over the front of her from her neck all the way down between her legs, over her clothes. She leans into my touch like a cat.

"You need to be naked, Chloe Jane, I want to memorize every last detail of this perfect body of yours." I take my time looking her over as I reach behind her and unhook her bra, peeling it from her body slowly. Her skin is the color of rich cream, her breasts heavy and rose tipped, shaped perfectly to slightly overflow my hands when I cup them. Her breathing goes shallow, her eyes holding mine as my hands explore her body.

I mouth over her chest, sucking, biting and kissing until she's breathing in short little pants, her hands clutching my hair. After I've memorized the taste and texture of her breasts, I set Chloe on her feet in front of me. She wobbles a little at first and I wrap my arms around her to hold her up until she stabilizes. When her knees finally lock, I let her go. I look her over top to bottom, slowly perusing her body. She shivers, her eyes hot on me.

Hooking my fingers in the waistband of her leggings, I tug them down her legs, following their descent with my mouth. She braces her hands on my shoulders and whimpers when my tongue delves between her legs after I remove her teal lace panties. My hands are firm on her hips, to help keep her steady while I take my time exploring her silky folds, tasting her arousal. I don't stop until her fingernails have pierced the skin on my shoulders and she's shaking, gasping out my name.

I pull her close, letting her collapse into me. She's still working on regaining her breath, and I kiss her, stealing it again. Chloe presses her body against mine, all soft curves, big green eyes and heat and I decide we've gone slow enough for tonight.

Chloe

THE RESIDENTS OF WHITE OAK, NEW YORK HAVE NEVER BEEN known for their reticence. Word spreads fast that Raif and I are dating. In days, I'm overwhelmed by abrupt silences when I walk into a room. Don't they know how obvious that is? Do they not even care how rude they're being? Why can't they all just get a life and mind their own business? It's hard for me to enjoy my happiness at knowing Raif shares my feelings when it seems like I'm exploring this new adventure while living under a microscope. Raif doesn't seem to care one way or the other, but he doesn't know what it's like being Lilly May Morris's daughter.

He doesn't know that I feel the judgmental eyes of town matrons on everything I do, waiting for me to falter. Waiting to see me mess up and bring more shame on my family's name. Every day is a tightrope act for me as it is. He has never understood that pressure. And I don't want him to, I wouldn't wish this feeling on anyone.

It's not like we've shouted on street corners that we're in love. But Raif kissing me in front of Hank Warner, the bored old gossip, was enough to set their tongues wagging. I haven't seen Violet Montgomery yet to assess any damage I might have caused with her. I know that as Raif's best friend, Vi loved me. She was supportive and motherly and plain old wonderful to me. But this is different. I'm the daughter of the town whore/drug addict. No woman wants their son to end up with someone with my family ties.

"I can feel you stressing from here, Chloe Jane." I startle at Raif's voice. And then he's wrapping his arms around me from behind, pulling me up against his chest. The skirt of my sundress swirls around both our legs as he envelops me in the warmth and comfort of his arms, the smell of his cologne lightly scenting the air around us. He rests his chin on top of my head. "I'm telling you, everything is going to be fine."

My heart clenches in my chest, I hope he's right. Today is Vi's annual end-of-summer cook out. Our first real public appearance as a couple. His nonchalance is giving me a migraine, but to be fair, my overthinking is probably making him just as nuts. "I can't help it." I say, my eyes on the fruit salad I'm preparing to bring with us.

Raif squeezes me closer, and I have a moment of disbelief that this is real. He loves me. We're together. Could it really be that easy?

"Darlin', I know you think I don't understand, but I do live here, too. And I do know my mom. She adores you. You have nothing to worry about."

"Have you talked to her about us?"

"Well. No. I didn't think she'd want to hear about all the details." His beard tickles my neck as he drops a soft kiss there.

"Be serious, please?" I beg him while tilting my head and giving him better access to my ear. He hugs me tighter, kissing my cheek and resting his chin on my shoulder.

"Honey, I am. Mom and I have talked about my love life exactly twice and that was only because she was worried about me. All Mom's gonna care about is that we're both happy."

"I hope you're right." I shudder, my stomach dipping unpleasantly at the thought of Violet's wrath being directed at me. Or at Raif, because of me. Raif blows a raspberry on my neck and swats me on the behind.

"Enough worrying, woman, let's get going. I told Mom we'd help set up."

I laugh, smiling at him. He's so free compared to a month ago. *I did that*, I realize. *I make him happy*.

I square my shoulders and let the happiness fill me up, too, bolstering me for whatever might come next. I wrestle a sheet of plastic wrap over the bowl of fruit salad and deem it and myself ready to go. "You're right." He smiles at me, another wide smile that lights up his eyes. He kisses me sweetly. "All set," I tell him, and I mean it now.

"I'll get this," he offers, grabbing the heavy bowl before I can object. I allow the chivalry and grab my bag, slinging it over my shoulder, leading the way to my door.

We take Raif's Jeep even though Vi's house is only a few blocks away. Definitely close enough that we could have walked. We probably would have if we hadn't been bringing food and other supplies. When we arrive, we park down the block, so we won't be boxed in by the other guests later. I knock on the front door and Daisy, Raif's 18-year-old sister opens the door and squeals.

"You're here!" She bounces forward and grabs me in a bear hug, her blonde curls flying everywhere in her excitement. I hug her back, grinning happily.

"We're here," I reply, rubbing her back. "How've you been, Daisy? It's been too long since I saw you."

She pulls me inside, looping her arm around my waist and resting her head against mine, she's about an inch taller than me but loves being cuddled. "I know! You are always working, Chloe, you need to take some time off and come visit. Mom and I both miss you."

I squeeze her against me and sigh. "I know, sugarplum, I miss you, too. But I have bills to pay, and I can't let the Saloon fail. Merle would rise up from the grave to murder me."

Raif sighs dramatically. "I see I'm as invisible as always when you two get together."

"Hush, you. I'll get to you in a minute," Daisy says, leading us through the house. The rooms are as familiar to me as my own. "But Chloe, do you like ever stop and think about what you want? Or is it all just family duty and bills to pay?"

I stiffen at her words. I know she's not trying to upset me, but she's right. I can't remember the last time I really thought about what I want from life. I've been in survival mode for as long as I can remember.

Raif chastises his sister. "Tact, Daise. Get some." Immediately, I feel the younger girl tense under my arm.

"I'm sorry, Chloe. I didn't mean it in a bad way." Daisy sounds like she might cry at her brother's admonition.

"No, it's alright," I insist. "It's a valid question."

Raif looks saddened by my words, like maybe he didn't realize my mindset. I force a smile and tell him. "I'm okay, cupcake." I kiss Daisy's cheek and ruffle her curls. "It's fine." I murmur to her softly when I note the tremble in her lips. She throws herself in my arms and hides her face in my neck just like when she was 6 and scraped her knee trying to climb a tree with her brother and me. I let her hide for a moment, knowing how she struggles with disappointing people. It sets off a chain reaction of panic and fear in her.

I look at Raif and say, "Heya cupcake, how about you bring that fruit salad to the kitchen and let Vi know we're here?" I know right now his sister needs a few moments of peace to breathe and get her bearings.

He looks sad as he runs a hand over Daisy's curls lovingly. Dropping a quick kiss on my mouth, he mouths the words, "Thank you." He pulls back and speaks out loud this time. "Good idea, darlin'. I'll see you ladies in the backyard in a few."

I wait until her brother is gone, and then kiss the top of Daisy's curly head. "Deep breaths in and out, sweetheart."

She glances up at me, a crestfallen cherub, and frowns. "Is it true you and Raif are *dating?*" She's flushed from her episode, her hands still trembling.

I gnaw on my bottom lip, worried about how she's going to take this news. "Is that okay with you?"

A small eternity passes before she grins, more like herself. "Chloe, are you kidding? *Of course* it's okay with me. You're good for him. I'm just surprised. I always thought you and Luke..." She lets the sentence trail off when I shake my head.

"No, Luke and I are better as friends." I say, which is true. Daisy nods at my words looking thoughtful.

"I guess you're right. I mean, he would've made his move by now, right? If he was gonna, I mean."

"I'd think so, yes." I say, trying to stop from rolling my eyes at her. It's just so ludicrous to think that Luke would be carrying a torch for me after all this time.

Daisy huffs at me. "I can tell you don't believe me, just so you know." She sounds miffed at me and I can't hold back a laugh.

"I'm sorry. I am, it's just hard for me to imagine." I hug her again.

Clearly, I'm forgiven because she allows it. "That's because you have no idea how awesome you are."

I shrug wordlessly and wait a beat. "How're you doing?"

"I'm fine now." She sounds embarrassed, so I allow her to drop the subject.

"Okay," I keep my tone light. "Ready for some fun?"

She nods, grinning at me again, and we link arms to go out to the backyard where classic rock music is already blaring from a stereo system. Vi is directing Raif on where to move one of the picnic tables. They already look to be arranged in my opinion. They're in a sort of circle, so everyone can see everyone else. Vi is big on making sure everyone can talk and have fun together, so no one feels left out.

"Raif, no, no, to the right, honey." Violet says, arranging flowers in a vase on one of the tables. She's the same height as Daisy, and she looks more like her older sister than her mother. Her hair is the same length and just a shade darker than Daisy's. Right now, it's twisted up and away from her tanned face. She's a classic beauty, dressed in a pair of denim shorts and a pink tank top.

Raif mumbles something incoherent but does as instructed. Daisy and I laugh and Vi looks up, her smile breaking across her face like a rainbow after a thunderstorm when she sees us. "There's my two favorite women on the planet."

Relief floods my chest and I smile wider. "Right back atcha. How can we help?"

"You can hug me, stranger." Vi comes skipping over to us and grabs me up in a hug that could crack my ribs. I don't mind. I hug her back just as hard. "I'm so happy you two have finally figured things out." Vi says quietly and I feel tears prick at my eyes.

"Me, too." I murmur in response, trying to keep my emotions in check.

She rubs my back and says, "This is how it should have been all

along, sweet tart. I knew it in my gut. You brighten my boy."
Immensely relieved, I pull back from her and find Daisy looking
very smug next to us.

"Of course I heard." She says before her mother can ask, and I
laugh at her sassy attitude. Swiping at my eyes, I take a breath, let
myself believe that everything really is going to be alright. Raif
catches the motion and turns laser eyes on the three of us.

"Okay, what are you two doing to my girl? No making her cry. I
told her everything would be okay. Are you trying to make a liar out
of me now?" He is at my side and running his thumbs over my
cheeks to check for any lingering tears in a heartbeat. He leans down
and kisses my mouth. "What'd they do, darlin'? You know I'd slay
any dragon for you."

I smile up at him, overcome by how lucky I feel, how happy I am
that he loves me, that I can have this. "They were happy tears,
cupcake. Stow your sword and remember I'm no damsel in distress. I
can slay dragons all on my own."

"Yes, I know you can." He says, his deep, rich voice serious. "But
you don't have to, Chloe Jane. Never again."

Raif

CHLOE'S NERVOUSNESS SEEMS TO HAVE MELTED AWAY WITH MY mother's hug. There's no longer any tension in any part of her as she smiles and laughs with everyone. Currently she's singing karaoke with my sister. *Girl in a Country Song* by Maddie and Tae. Daisy is tone deaf and could make dogs cry with her falsetto voice. Chloe, on the other hand, has a husky alto voice that belongs behind a microphone.

There've been many times I've tried to get her to sing with us, but she's always claimed she'll leave the singing to the true talents. She just doesn't see that she *is* a talent. The girls finish their song to lots of applause, they both curtsey to us, accepting their accolades. Chloe comes back to me with an extra little spring in her step. She looks so happy, her pretty yellow sundress swirling around her legs when I spin her into my arms and hug her.

"You are amazing." I tell her, sitting down and pulling her onto my lap.

She giggles at me, blushing. "Thanks, I thought we sounded pretty okay. And it was fun."

I hold her to me, drop a kiss on her bare shoulder and whisper in her ear, "You are amazing."

She blushes hotter and hides her face in my chest. I grin, caught up for a moment in how happy I am with her in my arms. I kiss the top of her head and look up to find my mother watching us with a soft smile on her face. I smile at her and she returns her attention to her best friend, Paige Benson, Luke's mother.

From across the yard, Troy's voice rings out, "But really, Daise. I love you and everything, but you should never sing again. Never. Not even in the shower." Chloe stiffens in my arms, going on the alert for signs of distress from my sister.

Daisy pouts at him, her cheeks rosy with embarrassment but before she can say anything, Luke speaks up. "Don't be a dick, Waters." The formerly happy gathering goes silent for a few beats. Luke doesn't normally lose his temper. Ever. Lately, though, his usual grin and easygoing attitude have been missing.

Troy frowns at him, but speaks to Daisy, "You know I was kidding, right, sweetheart?" his voice is unusually gentle for him. I know he didn't mean anything by it or I would've been all over him. Or Chloe would, she doesn't let anyone mess with people she loves. Luke's the one looking embarrassed now.

Daisy nods, sticking her chin in the air, her cheeks still a bit pink. "Of course." She glares good-naturedly at Troy. "It was still quite mean of you, though."

I grin. That's Daisy all over. She goes to Luke and hugs him. "Thanks for looking out, brother number two."

"Anything for you, doll face." Luke says. He looks at Troy, "Sorry." But Troy just shrugs it away. Typical Troy. Luke looks uncomfortable now, though. I look down at Chloe and find her watching him with a frown on her pretty face.

Mom stands up and claps her hands. "That'll be enough of all that, I think." Smiling, she gathers up the empty serving platters in front of her. "I think we're ready for desserts." She bustles into the house and I kiss Chloe's cheek to get her attention off of Luke. He doesn't need her overly analytical brain worrying over his behavior.

Chloe looks at me, her green eyes worried but gets up off my lap. "I'm gonna help," she says, laying a kiss on my lips before sashaying away from me. I enjoy watching her go for a moment and then shake myself out of it. I also rise, going over to Luke and sitting next to him. Bran is across the table from us, also looking mildly concerned. Not everyone is as clueless about nuances as Troy is. I put a hopefully comforting hand on Luke's shoulder. "You okay, brother?" I ask quietly.

Luke huffs at me, again, not in character for him and I remove my hand in response. "I'm fine." He answers after a moment, lifting his can of Guinness and draining it before setting it back down. When nothing else is forthcoming, Bran raises an eyebrow at me, his dark eyes worried. I shrug one shoulder. Bran sighs and shakes his dark head.

Luke growls at us. "When did you two become a couple of hens worrying over their baby chick? And when the fuck did I become your baby chick?"

Troy laughs but he's the only one. Bran clears his throat and murmurs, "Uh, when you started taking people's heads off for having a little fun...that's when I became a... Hen, you said?"

Luke nods after a moment. "Okay then, I suppose I have to accept that." He stands and sighs. "I'mma take a walk. I'll see you tomorrow."

I look at him silently for a moment then murmur. "Make sure you say goodbye to the girls or we'll never hear the end of it." He nods before he escapes into the back door of my mother's house.

Bran glances at me once Luke's inside and asks, "Is he okay?" He sounds nervous and I don't blame him. Luke's the steadiest of us all. Normally. But nowadays he's a surly bear that stomps around town looking like he wants to hit things.

"I don't know." I admit, because it's true. "We'll keep an eye on him."

Mom and Chloe come back out with their arms laden down with bowls and such and Bran and I both get to our feet to help them lighten their loads. Mom unloads the bowl of fresh whipped cream into Bran's waiting arms, "Oh, thank you, Brandon. Such a gentleman."

Chloe glares at me. "You can just sit yourself back down, Raif. I'm *fine*." But she's clearly overloaded with the heavy bowl of fresh sugared strawberries cradled in her right arm, and the tray of home-made shortcakes balanced on her left hand. I know she was a wait-ress before she took over running the Saloon, but I can't help worrying that she's going to lose her burdens at any moment. "I mean it." She reiterates as I hover by her side to catch anything that might fall.

"I know you mean it, and you're fearsome as all get out. I'm just being cautious. It would be a shame to lose Paige's delicious treats." She shoots daggers at me out of her eyes once more and I hold my hands up, staying a step behind her, just in case.

She sets down her cargo and turns to me, small hands planted on the hips I love hanging on to. Her green eyes flash dangerously at me. "You are impossible, you know that?"

I grin at her, flashing my teeth and pull her into my arms, keeping her right up against me. "I know, I'm awful." I kiss her full on the mouth, ignoring our crowd of onlookers. She's pliant against me when I pull back a few moments later, there may be some whistling from our friends. I don't care. All I care about is Chloe. Her mouth hovers inches from mine, still open, as we share breaths.

"Impossible man." She says again and kisses me once more.

I allow it for a moment and then pull back to say against her mouth, "But you love me." My grin is wide, daring hers to come out and play and she obliges.

Eyes open, smiling into mine, she kisses me again, then says. "I do indeed."

The next day, after Chloe leaves for work, I make my way to Luke's apartment. I hate how upset he is. More than that, I hate that I'm part of the reason he's so miserable right now. I've never wanted to hurt anyone, especially not one of my very best friends. If I thought it would help, if it wouldn't break Chloe's heart and my own, I'd try and end our relationship. But it's too late for that now and honestly, I don't know if I'm strong enough to pull it off anyway.

Now that Chloe and I have begun dating, now that I've told her how I feel, kissed and touched her and slept with her in my arms all night long, I'd never be able to give her up. Not for anything in the world. I'm smart enough to know that I'm better with her than I've ever been without her. She makes me a better man. Stronger and more complete. I could never let her go. Not even for Luke.

I knock on Luke's door around noon, but there's no answer. I sigh. I was worried this might happen. I take out my key to his apartment and unlock the door, opening it and poking my head inside. "Luke? You home, brother?"

His car is in the spot in front of the building, but the air inside smells stale like he hasn't opened his windows in a few days at least. And maybe the garbage hasn't been taken out in a week. This is troublesome. Luke is not your typical bachelor, he's clean and orderly in his home. Borderline obsessive about it. He says he simply takes pride in his small space, because it is his own. That could be. Or it could've just been ingrained in him by his three older sisters.

Luke's the youngest in his family, and the only boy. His sisters helped teach him about how to treat a woman, how to be a good man, how to change the oil in his car. Everything a father should have taught him, his sisters stepped up and taught him instead. His mother was too deeply buried in grief to be much help. Her husband had died of a massive coronary when Luke was only four.

I call out again, worried at the way my voice is echoing around the small space. "Luke? C'mon, man, make a noise, please."

I hear a low groan, a sound of pain, and I frown. I fully enter the apartment and shut the door behind me. Luke barely ever gets drunk, never so drunk that he's hungover the following day. He believes in moderation in all things. Knowing he must be in rough shape, I go to the kitchen first, grab a glass of water and the aspirin. Then I make my way to the bathroom where I find Luke retching into the toilet. He's shaking and sweating, his body racked with spasms and I set the water and medicine on the counter. I grab a washcloth and wet it with cool water from the tap.

Luke finishes vomiting and rests against his bathtub for support. I hand him the washcloth. "Here." He takes it without speaking, mopping the mess from his face and then dropping the dirty cloth behind him in the empty bathtub. He rests his hand wearily over his closed eyes. "Luke," I start. "I'm worried for you, man. This isn't like you."

Luke grumbles at me. "Don't you have an old lady to help cross the street or somethin'?" He doesn't move his hand, doesn't try and move off the floor. "I will be fine, Raif. Just had some fun last night s'all."

"Yeah, looks like you had a blast." I murmur, leaning against the open bathroom door and observing my friend.

"You are judging me aren't you? And that's just nonsense because not three weeks ago, you were way worse than I am right now. You didn't even know the names of the girls you were dipping your dick into. That means you don't get to judge. Even if you are lucky enough to call Chloe yours now." His voice is wrecked, and his barbs strike true.

I work to control my temper. "Luke, I'm not saying I don't deserve your anger, I know I do." I swallow hard, trying to ignore the feeling of panic, of loss at the idea of not having Chloe anymore. "If I'd known that you felt this way, I wouldn't have started anything with her, I would've left it alone. I swear."

Luke's hand moves now, as he lurches half off the floor, his voice enraged. "You ass, I'm not mad that she's happy!" He's up and in my face, his two-inch height advantage suddenly glaringly obvious. "I knew I didn't have a shot. I knew in high school! I knew how she felt about you, maybe before she did. But I also didn't think you were ever gonna get your head right and get rid of that bitch you were with. And I couldn't stop loving her. I tried. Trust me." His voice breaks on his last words. He leans back against his sink, seemingly exhausting his rage along with his energy.

"Luke, I'm sorry you're hurting." I say after a few moments of ashamed silence on my end. I should have known he wasn't angry at me for making her happy. No, he's just mourning what he knows he won't ever have. It's real now that she's never gonna be his again, and that's a pain I cannot even imagine. I don't know if I'd survive it if I was the one in his shoes right now.

I try to picture it; Luke and Chloe together now, after I realized how deep my love for her runs. Seeing them together, his hands on her, kissing her. Her laughing up at him, sharing his bed, his life. It turns my blood cold, slows my heart down to a stuttering crawl in my chest. My hands start shaking and I fist them to hide it. "How can I help?"

Luke snorts. Shakes his head and then groans again, grasping his head in his hands. "You can't, Raif. No one can do anything." His voice is quiet, filled with pain. "You should just go."

Chloe

"Luke, open up. I know you're home. I see your tiny little hybrid thing out here on the street." I bang loudly on the front door three more times. I hear vague grumbling and movement from within.

Since Luke's strange behavior at Vi's cookout last week, I have been trying to watch him closer. I'm worried for him; he's withdrawn, sullen and silent. None of which is normal for him. Renegades are scheduled to play another show at the Saloon tomorrow night and I know that Dell Xander will be making another appearance, because I invited him. The guys need to be at the top of their game this time. I think he could be interested in them, even though they are all certain Raif wrecked their shot with his bullheadedness. This is the excuse I'm using to butt into whatever issue Luke is currently having. I'm worried, like I said, and this is just not like him.

"Luke!" I bellow again, my fist pounding some more.

The door opens finally, and Luke stands there glaring at me impressively. He's shirtless, his broad shoulders are tense, his normally bright blue eyes bloodshot. "Sweet tart, what on earth are you doing out here screeching like a banshee?" He's practically growling, and I raise my chin and glare right back at him.

"I'm checking in on my friend. Like you've done for me a thousand times. Now step aside and let me in. I can smell your garbage from here. You're clearly in the midst of some kind of crisis. Let me help, damn it!"

He stares me down for a few seconds, but I cross my arms over my chest and glare back at him. Eventually, he groans and steps aside.

"Fine. Come in. You are not cleaning my house, though. I'm not your boyfriend. I don't need you to pick up after me." There's a definite bite to his voice that's not normally present and I stiffen.

"Gee, with a welcome like that, how can I say no." I huff at him. "And I know you're not Raif. What the hell is your problem, Luke Benson? You don't have to be my boyfriend for me to be worried, to check in on you!" I poke him in the chest with my finger. "I don't appreciate your tone."

"I'm sorry," he grumbles, moving back from me. Probably to mask the scent of stale Guinness that's hanging around him like a foul cologne. This is not Luke. He's usually better put together than I am. I look him over closer, his eyes are bloodshot and hooded. His normally perfectly coiffed hair is greasy, his beard wild. I frown.

"Luke..." I take a step toward him, but he steps back.

"Nope, you don't want to get any closer, Chloe." He holds his hands up in front of him as if to ward me off, and I try not to be hurt at the obvious rejection of any sort of physical contact. He needs a hug, I can tell. I know him just as well as I know Raif, as well as I know myself.

I go to him despite him trying to keep me back and I hug him, despite his stiffness. I pat his back and say, "Whatever is going on, it's going to be okay, I promise. Let me help. Please?"

He sighs after a second and I feel him slump in on himself. He hugs me hard and buries his face in my hair, then abruptly, but gently pushes me back. He clears his throat. "I'm okay, but I stink... uh." He sounds sad, so sad; and again, that's so unlike him.

I try to grab his gaze. "Luke, it's okay. Why don't you go take a shower, I'll put the kettle on for some tea?"

He nods woodenly and swallows, his eyes on the floor. "I.... Yeah, that's a good idea." He starts to turn towards the bathroom and turns back to me at the last second, pointing his finger at me. "I meant it though, no cleaning my house. It's my mess. I'll fix it."

I nod silently at him, even though we both know the moment the water goes on in that shower, I'm gonna start picking things up out here. I can't stand to be still and just look at it like this.

He nods and escapes into the bathroom, and as soon as I hear the shower start, I turn to get cleaning supplies. I find the tea kettle and check for cleanliness before filling it with water and setting it on the stovetop. I find one of his mother's coffee cakes defrosting in the fridge and put it out on the counter. I open all the windows wide, turn the stereo on and WGNA, our local country station blares to life from the speakers. I turn it down to a dull roar and start clearing away the mess. When Luke emerges from the bathroom with a towel wrapped around his hips fifteen minutes later, he growls at me. "Damn it, Chloe. I told you no."

"And you knew I wouldn't listen," I counter. "Hush and go get dressed."

He growls again. "Impossible woman!" But he moves towards his bedroom to get dressed just the same.

"And proud of it." I mutter as I load up his dishwasher with the dirty dishes I collected from around his apartment. I change the overflowing garbage bag and carry it to the front door to live until I make Luke bring it outside. By the time he comes out of his bedroom dressed in a dark blue tee shirt and blue jeans, I've got the place mostly sorted out.

Luke looks around the formerly wrecked apartment and shakes his head. "Well, you're nothing if not efficient, sweet tart."

I stick my tongue out at him. "Why waste time when I'm here and able bodied?"

"You know why. My mess, I fix it." I frown at him, studying his face. He looks a little better now that he's clean, at least. He smells much better, too. I wish I knew what was going on in his head. Luke's always been so unflappable. And a good friend to me whenever I've needed him.

"Would you come here, please?" I ask, pulling the coffee cake out of the oven where it's been warming to take the chill off. I set it on the counter and look back and see Luke actually listened. He's behind me, leaning against his counter with his arms stuffed in the pockets of his jeans. He looks uncomfortable. Again, all new things.

I turn around and face him, and he holds my eyes for a beat, his shoulders loosening a bit, his jaw unclenching for the first time in a week. "Thank you for your help."

I shrug one shoulder. "I'm always here to help if you need it. And you've helped me often enough in the past. Can you tell me what's up? I'm scared for you, Luke."

He smiles at me, a real smile, but it's sad. "Naw, you don't want to hear it, honey. I swear I'm okay. Or okay, I *will* be okay. Just going through some stuff is all. It happens to us all from time to time. Right?"

I worry my lower lip between my teeth while I watch his face, looking for any signs of dishonesty. But there aren't any because this is Luke and he doesn't lie. "First off, Luke Benson, I want to hear anything you need to get off your chest. I know I'm not one of the guys, but I love you like a brother, you know that."

He grins, but it still looks sad to me. "I know you do. And I love you back. C'mere and hug me like I know you wanna. I can see it in your eyes."

"Don't be a know-it-all." I sass but I do as he says, crossing to him and burrowing into the front of him, scared for some reason. He wraps his strong arms around me and holds me to him, but it's off. I feel like something's changed between us and I missed it. I don't understand why it's happening, but I've hurt Luke somehow. And that's something I swore I would never do again when I broke up with him back in our junior year of high school.

Normally Luke will hold me for ages, never complaining, but now he lets his arms drop after just a few moments. I step back and swallow down unexpected tears. He's watching my face like always, studying me for signs of distress. But his easy manner, his affection for me is gone. Somehow, this is my fault. And it all clicks in my head as I watch his eyes shutter to me for the first time ever. He stuffs his fists back in his pockets and I take another step back from him.

Daisy was right.

I open my mouth and close it again, I have no idea what to say to him right now. And I don't want to start crying and make him feel worse than he does. He has every right to keep his distance from me to help himself. I never thought in a million years that sweet, handsome Luke would still care for me this way.

But I can see it now, in the way he's distancing himself. I never thought it would hurt this much to get what I wanted. Everything always carries a price. I should have learned this lesson by now. But I never thought I'd lose Luke. He's been a fixture in my life for almost as long as Raif.

Would I have thrown myself into my relationship with Raif if I'd known what I'd be giving up? I don't know for sure, and that scares me more. All I know for certain is I don't want anyone else to get hurt.

I paste a fake smile on my face while my heart aches. "Okay well, you should be good to go here. Let me know if you need anything. Or want to talk." In trying to be normal, I'm exacerbating my awkwardness, but it can't be helped now. I blink the tears from my eyes and look up at him, my bottom lip clamped between my teeth. "I gotta go. I'll see you around."

He doesn't stop me.

I never warned the guys that Dell is coming to their show. I figure it will only make them nervous and they don't need that pressure. Things will be better this time. When the band arrives at 7:30, I am four people deep at the bar, making drinks. We are slammed. It's like everyone in town knows that a big-time record producer is coming to watch the boys play, and they all want a front row seat.

Raif grins when he sees me, and I return it while noting that Luke's usual wave isn't forthcoming. *It's fine,* I tell myself. *Everything will be fine.* I keep my smile on my face, glad that Raif decides not to come say hello in person since we're so busy. I don't want him getting the wrong idea. I return my attention to the customers clamoring for drinks and the boys start setting up.

Dell shows up after I've cleared out the waiting customers and sits at the same stool as last time. Smiling, he slides me a five-dollar bill, "Club soda please, Chloe. Thanks again for the invite."

I make change and offer up a bowl of pretzels for him to snack on while he waits. "You're welcome. Thanks for coming back. I promise you won't be sorry."

He sips his drink and nods at me. "We'll see," he retorts, but he's smiling.

I leave him at the bar to go up on stage at eight pm sharp. I smile out at the crowd and clap my hands before leaning in and saying, "Are you all having a good time?" The applause picks up and a few people shout out a resounding 'Yes' in response. I laugh, "Good! Keep on drinking. And put your hands together for our very own Renegades!" I look back at the band, "Take it away, boys!" And then I exit the stage as Troy counts them down with his drum kit.

I can feel eyes on me as I move back to the bar and I keep a smile on my face despite my inner turmoil. The boys start their set with an old reliable cover of Cole Swindell's *Let Me See Ya Girl*. The crowd loves it and I see Dell tapping his foot along with the rest. I relax and trust in my boys. I know they can impress this producer.

They make their way through a few more covers and then Raif surprises me. "Chloe Jane, you need to get your fine behind back up here, please. We need you for our next song."

I freeze in place and stare up at him, feeling the eyes of everyone in the Saloon glued to my face. Dell is grinning, "Threw you a curveball it seems," he says, and I nod, feeling my face heat.

Zora comes over to the bar to take over for me, her face glowing with her giant smile. She nudges me out from behind the bar. I sigh, accepting the inevitable and head to the stage. "Get on up here, darlin'." Raif says when he sees me dragging my feet. "Chloe and I wrote this song together and I really think she should be a part of performing it. We're gonna see what you all think about it tonight."

The crowd applauds and shrieks their approval as I ascend the steps to the stage. Raif is looking at me like he knows this might result in a fight later. I smile at him anyhow and he grins back, "Remember you love me," he says as I get closer to him, away from the microphone.

"We'll talk about it later." I murmur back to him. Luke hands me a microphone and gestures to a stool Bran brought up on stage for me to sit on. I take it and sit down where they want me.

"All right, this is called *Only You*. We hope you like it." Raif says as Luke starts in on the intro with his fiddle. Raif begins singing, his voice smooth and decadent, like fine whiskey and I close my eyes and let myself get lost in the song. It's a ballad but it's not slow, it's got an in-between tempo.

There's something you need to know
I thought for sure it would show
But you haven't seemed to notice my distraction
Maybe, when you touch me, you can't feel my reaction
I don't know but I can't stop smiling, thinking about you
So, baby, please don't give me a reason to

I join in with him for the chorus, keeping my eyes closed as we harmonize.

Cuz I can't stop this feeling and I don't wanna try
to keep my heart from soaring straight up to the sky
I want to bring you closer, show you how I feel
let you into the broken heart only you knew how to heal

I don't know what motivates me, but I know the next verse and when it's time for it to begin, I sing it without opening my eyes. Pretending that it's just Raif and me in my apartment or his house, him strumming the guitar while I sing out the lyrics we're writing.

My friends say I'm looking different
and I'm thinking you were heaven sent
How do I show you, show me what to do
Cuz I can't think straight, baby, when I'm with you

Raif never even starts so I'm guessing this was his plan all along. The fiddle's still playing, but everything else has stopped. And when the chorus is supposed to begin, I'm still singing on my own.

I can't stop this feeling and I don't wanna try
To keep my heart from soaring straight up to the sky
I want to bring you closer, show you how I feel
Let you into the broken heart only you knew how to heal
Raif's deep voice joins mine again on the final lines.
So I'll just be straightforward and tell you how I feel
I've let you in my broken heart only you knew how to heal

Luke plays the outro beautifully and I open my eyes when I hear the thunderous applause of the crowd. Raif's standing in front of me, facing me, not the crowd. His smile is brighter than ever, pride and happiness oozing out of him. This really meant a lot to him. He sweeps me off my stool and into his arms, kissing me soundly on the mouth. "I love you." He says softly, just for me.

Grinning and blushing, I step back from him, waving to the crowd. They're still applauding. *Wow.* Raif goes back to his microphone, "She's got a gorgeous voice, right y'all?" he says, and I wave him off but there are hoots and catcalls, still a ton of clapping.

I make my way off the stage, accepting high fives from Luke and Bran and a wink from Troy before I go. I head back to the bar, keeping my head down, but there are people patting me on the shoulder every few steps, calls of, "You were wonderful!" My face is possibly on fire, it's so hot.

Dell is still clapping when I get back behind the bar. Zora engulfs me in an enthusiastic hug. "Where have you been hiding that voice, girl?"

I duck my head again. "Oh, I'm not that good."

Zora bumps me with her hip, but before she can speak, Dell does. "Yes, you are, my dear." I look at him and a grin spreads over my face.

"Well, thank you." I murmur.

Raif is clapping along with the crowd, "Thank you, Chloe Jane, for lending us your beautiful presence."

I give a little bow from behind the bar. "Get on with your set, boys." I call, embarrassed by all the attention. Raif salutes me, and they launch into *Somethin' I'm Good at* by Brett Elderidge. I do my best to ignore the stares of my customers.

Raif

We finish our set to thunderous applause and I leave
the stage immediately to go put my arms around Chloe. I don't know if
she wants to slug me or hug me, but either way, I have to find out. She
was absolutely amazing. Fearless. Exactly as I knew she'd be if she'd
take the chance. I see her behind the bar, working her butt off, looking
sexy as sin in her painted-on jeans and red V-neck tee shirt. She has her
don't look at me face on, but I go around to the employee side of the bar
anyway. Regardless of the countless people in attendance watching
our every move, I pull her into my arms and kiss her breathless.

She's pliant against me immediately, kissing me back until her
hands are tugging at my hair and the people around us are clapping
and catcalling for more. She steps back suddenly, her eyes fever

bright, her cheeks pink, her mouth swollen from my kiss. I move towards her again, wanting her more than ever. She presses her hand to my chest to keep me a step away from her. All I want is to follow her heat, press her back against the office door behind us and taste her lips again.

"You know better than to spring something like that on me," she says, her voice quiet and shaky, despite her tiny grin.

I nod. "I'll take my punishment later, but I have to tell you, darlin', you were absolutely amazing. I promise." She blushes hotter and shoves my shoulder.

Dell Xander speaks up from the other side of the bar. "Any chance I can get a sit down with you fellas?" I look up at him, surprised to see him sitting there. I guess I might have tunnel vision on Chloe.

"I'm pretty sure we can make that happen," I tell him. He smiles and leaves a ten-dollar bill on the bar for Chloe. "Can we borrow your office, Chloe Jane?" I ask her.

She glances between us and nods. "Of course you can." She looks flustered still and I grin down at her, wanting badly to ignore the record producer and go somewhere quiet to have a conversation with my girl about her performance earlier.

Before I can pull her away, though, the rest of the band is crowding around Chloe at the bar. Troy tugs her too far away from me and scoops her up in a hug. "Dude!" he crows at her, hugging her until she laughs. "You were fanfuckingtastic!" He spins her a bit and then sets her down.

When Bran takes a turn, hooking his arm around her shoulders and pulling her into his chest, she's still laughing. I love the sound of her laughter probably more than any other in the world. "You really were, honey." Bran tells her.

She steps back from Bran and beams up at them both, "Thanks boys. It was a lot of fun."

I notice Luke's eyes are glued to Chloe's face, the smile plastered across it. He steps forward when Chloe finally swings her eyes to his. Normally, he would have been the first one around the bar, after me. They look almost awkward right now, Chloe pulling on her hands and Luke rubbing the back of his neck. But finally, he pulls her into his arms, cradling her head against his chest, burying his face in her hair. I can't hear what he says, but I see Chloe's arms tighten around him in response. They hold each other for a long moment and I see Chloe swipe her fingers under her eyes fast when they pull apart.

Seeing that moment sends anxiety coursing through me for a moment. Clearly, something's happened that I didn't know about. I knew Luke has been trying to keep a bit of a distance from Chloe for now until he moves through what he's feeling. But I didn't realize that Chloe figured that out. I can see pain on her face now and it tightens my chest, dries my mouth out. I want to hold her, make her forget whatever it is that put that look on her face. But Dell Xander takes that moment to insert himself into the scene.

"Hi there, guys. I'm glad you're all here. I'd really like to speak to you all." Dell gestures towards the closed office door and Chloe snaps to attention.

"Yes, yes. Go on in, I don't mind," she says, her eyes going back to the line at the bar once again. She frowns. "You guys can fill me in later if you'd like to," she murmurs finally, clearly disappointed.

Bran is the first through the office door, but I go to Chloe and lean down to kiss her mouth quickly. "I love you," I say quietly. "We can talk later?"

She smiles distractedly up at me and nods, jumping back into the fray and mixing drinks. "Course we can, cupcake. Get on in there. Don't keep Dell waiting."

I'm still distracted when I close the office door behind me and find the rest of the guys standing around, looking different levels of interested and concerned. Luke's hands are stuffed in his pockets, a sure sign of stress for him. Troy looks like he's not sure why we're in here but doesn't really care. Bran is rocking his poker face.

Dell grins at me when I enter, spreads his hands out in front of him. "Relax boys. It's good news. Or I think so, anyhow." I try to loosen my shoulders, watching Luke do the same. "I've heard your demo, I've seen you play three times now." I wonder when the third time was, but he continues. "I think Renegades are something special, and I'd like to produce a record or two with you." He looks around at us, gauging our reactions.

I study the other guys' faces, swallow down my nervous excitement. "I think I speak for all of us when I say I'd love to hear more."

Dell nods. "That makes sense." He meets each of our eyes for a nanosecond before he prattles on, as though he knows this pitch by heart. "As you know, I'm with Music City Records, based in Nashville, Tennessee. We would like to sign you boys to a two-album deal to begin with. Once we get you to Nashville to record, we'd have you meet with the marketing folks and figure out a plan for promoting you, touring, all that. You'd be in Nashville for probably three months, *minimum*, but honestly, most folks wind up getting a place there and staying. It's just easier."

My heart falls into my stomach and plummets all the way to my feet before coming back up to lodge itself in my throat. I open and close my mouth. Luke's the one who speaks first. "So leaving for an undetermined length of time." He clears his throat, looks around. "I think maybe the four of us should discuss this. Is there a number we can reach you at, set up a meet when we've had some time to think about things?"

Dell hums. "Sure thing. I'm staying about a half hour outside of town at the Best Western. I'll be here for another three days. You boys talk things over. I know you have families, jobs, other things to consider."

Bran speaks up. "Thanks, that would be great."

I keep my eyes trained on the record producer. It feels like I might be caught in a dream; one of the ones where I'm never sure if I'm having a nightmare or not. Dell looks me in the eye, "I hope you'll take us up on our offer guys. I think we could make something awesome together." He shakes all our hands before letting himself out of the office.

Troy speaks first once Dell's gone. "Well. What do we think?"

This is what we've all wanted forever, I know. But the timing is problematic. I want the record deal, I do. But I want Chloe more. She's my forever and I know it, but I don't know that she knows it yet. And I'm not ready to find out if I'm kidding myself and we have an expiration date. I'm not ready for the dream that is us to be over. How can I stand in the way of my brothers getting what they've always wanted? I have no idea what the hell I'm going to do.

"I think we should all think about it individually tonight," Bran says. "We can get together tomorrow morning and discuss it as a group then."

I nod, but Luke speaks before I can. "It's a plan. Be at mine at 10 and I'll make breakfast." And then he's leaving, not waiting for any of us to reply.

I sit at the bar, watching Chloe work, my mind going in a million different directions. She looks happy, carefree as she serves customers and then begins her closing routine. I watch her work, combing my fingers through my shaggy hair while I consider what I'm going to say to her once all the customers clear out. She keeps glancing over at me questioningly, clearly wondering what Dell wanted to talk to us about.

When Odetta waves goodbye to both of us and breezes out the door, Chloe locks it behind her and sighs. Leaning back against the closed door, she turns to me and smiles tiredly. "You have some explaining to do, cupcake. Come talk to me while I run reports."

I leave my bar stool and meet her at the end of the bar, pulling her into my arms and holding her to me for a few moments, silent and pensive. She lets me snuggle her close, her face pressed into my chest, her fingers playing in the hair at the nape of my neck. I breathe her in, trying to mentally prepare myself for this conversation. I'm not ready. I know I'm not ready. I could lose her right here. Easily. It could all slip through my fingers. The thought has my hands trembling, has me clasping her tighter to me.

"What's going on, Raif?" Chloe asks after a moment, her voice scared.

"Well, I have been dying to get you on stage with us, so I talked to the guys and we all decided tonight would be your debut." I begin.

She grunts to let me know that she heard me, waiting for me to continue. She looks up from my chest, her green eyes wary but patient. "What's the rest, cupcake?"

I memorize her face, the freckles dotting her creamy skin, the thick black lashes fringing her shining green eyes, the elf-like pointed chin. Her high cheekbones, full mouth. I run my knuckles over her face, just to feel the silk of her skin under my touch. She shivers but doesn't speak, still holding my eyes. Waiting me out.

I swallow. "Well, we got offered a record deal, Chloe Jane." The statement leaves a bowling ball of anxiety in my stomach.

Her face goes incandescent with happiness. "Really?!" she bounces in my embrace. "Oh, congratulations. I'm so proud of you guys, I knew you could do it. I knew it." Her eyes are wet with happy tears, joy radiating out of her. And then the other shoe drops. I see the curtain of uncertainty, of grief fall over her beautiful face. Watch the sunshine fade from her eyes. "Oh." She says finally, her voice shaky now. "Right."

"No decisions have been made, Chloe. I wouldn't do that to you. We decided to think tonight, on our own, talk tomorrow and discuss what we'd like to do."

She quirks a brow at me. "What's to think about, though, Raif? This has been the goal from day one..." she holds my gaze and shakes her head. "No. You are not giving this up for me. No. We can figure it out, right? I mean—" I watch her heart stumble and I cut her off, not willing to let her think I'd want out of this for even a moment.

I cup her face in my hands. "Stop. I'm not giving you up, Chloe. *No.* I don't want to be away from you. And this will mean moving to Nashville for at least a few months. Then possibly a tour, he said..." I swallow past the sudden lump in my throat. "I don't like when I can't wake up with you every morning as it is. We're just getting started and now I have to leave you?" Her hand comes up to touch my jaw, her eyes lost.

"I know. But it's not just about us, Raif. I can't let you turn down this opportunity. Not for me. I'm not gonna stop loving you just cuz you're not in town." Her voice catches, and she forces a slow breath out, licks her lips and smiles at me, but I see the pain. "You have to chase those dreams. You guys have come so far. Don't give up now. You deserve better."

I know she's right, no matter how much I hate it. I don't want to go. I would rather give up the band, figure out something else to do with my life, as long as it includes loving Chloe. But I know my girl. I know that she will blame herself if I don't do this. She will regret it on my behalf until it erodes everything that we are together. I can't let that happen.

I lean down, claiming her mouth with my own, kissing her with everything I feel for her, trying to convey the depth of my emotions in the kiss. She kisses me back, but I can taste the salt of tears, and I'm not sure which one of us is shedding them.

Chloe

Two weeks after Dell makes the offer to Renegades, I'm standing in Vi's basement. It now contains almost all of Raif's belongings that aren't making the trek to Nashville with him. He's giving up the rental house since the boys aren't sure how long they'll be gone. Why pay rent on an empty place? When the guys loaded up his bed into Bran's truck, I got misty eyed. I guess I had started to feel like his place was ours. His bed was my bed, and so on. I shouldn't have been presumptuous.

I feel like he's never coming back. Crazy, I know, but these are the thoughts that have been plaguing me. Even though I pushed for this, I hate that he's going. I feel like I'm being left behind. I mean, if he really didn't want to be without me, he would've asked me to come along. Or I'm overthinking. I can't be sure of anything anymore, and he hasn't even left yet. I hate feeling like this.

"Penny for your thoughts, Chloe Jane..." Raif says, his arms coming around me from behind. He pulls me back against his chest, crossing his arms tight around my hips.

I swallow hard. "It's just strange seeing it all here."

"It is that." He rests his chin on my shoulder. "I'm going to miss the house, I think. I didn't think I would. Thanks to you, though...lots of good memories there." He's rambling a little, he must be nervous. Bran will be picking him up and driving them to the airport in Albany, an hour away. They all asked their families not to come to the airport, he said. Make things easier, he said. I don't agree. I'll get to go to work and feel the ache of missing him like a toothache throbbing through my whole body.

I sigh, but don't speak. I'm afraid if I try, I'll start sobbing and begging him not to go and I can't do that. I can't be selfish. They have all worked so hard and they deserve this shot. He turns me around and frowns when his blue-green eyes meet mine. His touch skitters over my jaw, and I see pain in his eyes, too.

"You know I don't want to leave you, right?"

I nod, but still don't speak. He opens and closes his mouth, runs his fingers through the length of my ponytail. "I love you, Chloe. Say the word and I'll call Dell right now and take it all back. I'll stay here with you any day, darlin'. I need you to know that."

Tears swim in my eyes as I try to force out the words I know I have to say. He can't do that for me. I'm not worth it. And it's not fair to the other three. I choke down a sob and he pulls me into his chest. "I love you, too, but you can't stay now. You gave your word. I thought we'd talked about your white knight tendencies." My voice is muffled by the soft flannel of his shirt, but he understands.

"Chloe, I'd do anything for you, to hell with the rest of the world." He says into my hair. His arms are tight around me, holding me against him like I might disappear if he lets go. And let's be honest, when he lets go, he has only minutes until he's getting picked up. And he'll be the one disappearing.

I swallow down my tears, force a deep breath into my lungs and look up at him. "You have to go. Doesn't matter if I'll miss you like crazy." My voice wobbles and tears still track down my cheeks. He grabs my face in his hands, leans down and kisses me like I'm the air he needs to keep breathing. I kiss him back with equal fervor, wanting to memorize the feeling of his mouth on mine, the rightness of it. Burn this moment on my brain for when he's gone and the loneliness sets in. I can already feel it hovering around me, waiting to attack when he leaves.

I clutch at his shoulders, holding him against me, his hands find their way into my hair, pulling strands free from my already messy ponytail. He has me back against the wall, his body pressed right against mine, his mouth still owning mine when we hear someone coming down the basement stairs. I hear Luke clear his throat and pull my mouth from Raif's, my breath stuttering out of me in pants.

Raif's mouth comes back down on mine again; once, twice, three times, nibbling at my lips, exploring the inside of my mouth with quick sweeps of his tongue and I allow it. This is his goodbye, I know. When he pulls back this time, he rests his forehead against mine, his hands still on my face.

Luke sounds sincere when he says, "I'm sorry, guys. It's time. We'd better get on the road."

I make to move back but Raif won't let me go, he kisses me again. "I love you, Chloe. We'll talk all the time. We'll make this work."

I close my eyes for a moment, wanting so badly to believe him. "I love you, too." I say quietly, trying to stop crying. I open my eyes and find his watching me closely, and I try to smile at him. "We'll be okay. Let me know when you get to Albany."

He swallows, nods at me and steps back slowly, like it's causing him physical pain to leave me. I can feel Luke's eyes on us as Raif walks backwards until he's next to our friend. Luke frowns at me. "Do you want me to send Vi down?" He asks as he steers Raif towards the stairs.

I shake my head. "I'll be up in a minute. I just need to..." I swallow my excuse. "No, I'll be okay." I try again.

Luke looks back at me and nods. "Okay, sweet tart." He watches me for a long moment and then leaves Raif by the stairs and comes over and pulls me into his arms. He hugs me fast and hard, holding me close to him, kissing the top of my head. "We'll look after him."

I smile up at him, lean up and kiss his cheek, "Look after yourself, too."

Luke smiles back at me, more himself than he's been in weeks. "I promise, I will." He reaches up as if to stroke my cheek and then lets his hand drop and follows Raif's earlier path away from me.

Raif waves, and I wave back at both of them. "Be safe," I say. "I love you." I blow him a kiss and watch as he walks away. I make my way to the bottom step and slump down onto it gracelessly. I hide my face in my hands and let myself cry for real. No matter how unreasonable someone else may find my fears, I can't help but feel like I've lost Raif.

I don't know how long I sit down there by myself crying. Eventually, though I hear more footsteps coming down the basement stairs and then a moment later, someone settles onto the step next to me. I feel a thin arm come around my shoulders and then my head is being pillowed against another female chest. The scent of gardenias is strong around me and I know it's Violet. She strokes her hand over my hair comfortingly. "Hush, sweet tart, it's gonna be okay. He'll be back."

I hug her back and sob into her t-shirt. "I've never been without him for any length of time." I admit what's been building inside me all day. "What if he never comes back, Vi? What if he gets down there and just realizes what a mess I am and decides to st-stay?"

Vi chuckles. "Oh honey. You're nuts." She kisses my head and pulls back to make me look at her. "My son has been in love with you for his whole life. You have to know that by now."

I look at her, noting her sincerity. But I can't get rid of this feeling. This ache that he's gone, and he won't be back. I frown at her. "I can't help it. No one stays, Vi." I have never said that out loud before, ever.

Her face softens, "Honey, I know that's been your experience, but you have to have some faith. You and Raif will be okay. And Daisy and I are here for you, you're not alone." She smooths my hair away from my face. "Deep breaths. You get to be a mess today because you love him, and this is gonna be hard. But when you walk out of here today, you're gonna woman up and keep it together. I know you can handle this," she says, not unkindly.

I nod, looking at her. "You're right," I lie. "I'll be fine." I know she means well, I know she's trying to help me bolster myself. Pump me up and all that. But Raif and Luke are my best friends in the world. Raif and the Saloon are pretty much my whole world. I have no idea what I'm going to do with myself without Raif or the other members of the band to worry over and take care of.

"I know I am," she crows. "Now come on upstairs and eat something before you go to work. You don't ever eat enough as far as I'm concerned." I let her mother me a bit and follow her upstairs. She's right about one thing, I do need to get it together. I will not let the whole town see me fall apart.

I find myself sinking over the next few days. It's crazy really, how quickly it comes on me. The utter loneliness. I had thought my grandfather's death was the hardest thing I would ever have to live through. He passed away five months and eight days ago. But I had Raif and Luke here to help me through that. This new aloneness leaves what I was feeling then in the dust. It was a tangle of grief and responsibilities. All I wanted was to honor Merle's wishes. He had been mother, father, grandfather, friend and guardian to me over the course of my life. I owed him everything.

No one was more surprised than me when his will was read. I figured he'd want the business sold, and for me to have his house. He left everything to me, though. The only stipulation to any of it was that he wanted me to keep the ban he'd placed on my mother ever entering the Saloon. He'd long ago given up on reaching his only child and wanted to be sure I wouldn't waste my time or money on trying to mend fences with her when he was gone.

He knew me well. I had never felt so alone before as I have since he died. I was rudderless; lost. And I did have a very brief moment where I wished hopelessly that I could've grieved with my mother for our loss.

Silly pipe dreams on my part. My mother didn't even attend her father's funeral. She showed up afterwards at the reception I held at the Saloon. She was drunk, possibly high; I couldn't tell. I was swathed too thickly in grief. She came stumbling in with some new man on her arm, bellowing about the place belonging to her now. Looking around, at the entire adult population of our *very* small town, I'd been horror struck and silent, my face flaming. This was her legacy, she was forever making a spectacle of herself and bringing shame to our family. Raif and Luke hustled her and her *date* out before she even had a chance to speak to me, though. I found it difficult to meet people's eyes for days afterwards as news of her most recent public fit trickled through town.

When Merle Morris passed away, he essentially left me alone in this world. Lilly May might still be walking the Earth, but she only ever cared about herself and her next fix, her next drink. Other than her two appearances at the Saloon, she had made no effort to reach out to me since the reading of my grandfather's will. And those were more about her getting a free drink than seeing me. Once she'd learned that she was completely excluded from the behests, she walked out of the reading of the will. She was waiting for me outside, though, and immediately tried to guilt me into going against her father's wishes. She wanted me to sign everything over to her. The memory still stings as much as it did when it first happened.

"Chloe, you're young, you can do anything. There's still a chance for you to get Luke to give you another shot. He'll take care of you. You don't *need* a bar. What are *you* gonna do with it? It's not like you know how to run it." Her lack of faith in me was nothing new, her voice a raspy whine as she leaned too close, letting me smell the tequila on her breath.

I winced at the stench and stepped back from her, shaking my head at her ridiculous statement. "You don't get it. Merle didn't want anything of his to be left to you." Her vivid red-painted lips thinned, and I pressed on. "He didn't trust you not to burn the place down." There would be no sugarcoating anything for her, no smoothing things over. She wouldn't understand no matter what I said, and I knew that. "What you think of me doesn't matter, it's about what he wanted. Go sleep it off before you embarrass yourself worse."

I went to turn and leave but her hand flashed out and slapped me hard across the face, making my head snap back, the settings on the cheap rings she wore ripping the flesh of my cheek. "You've always been a selfish little bitch. You poisoned my parents against me." Two points of color stood out on her sunken cheeks, deepening the flush of her overdone cosmetics. She'd been beautiful once, with long silky dark hair and big grey eyes. Before the years of drugs, drinking and too many cigarettes had roughened her, sucking all the vitality out of her, leaving her a dried-up husk of a woman.

Before I'd even had the time to respond to her false accusations, she'd fled the scene. I stood there a moment with my hand covering what would be a fat lip and nasty looking cuts and bruises on my face the next day. Then, feeling more alone than I ever had before in my life, I squared my shoulders and sought refuge in the quiet of the still closed Saloon.

I shake myself out of the memories. I got through it. But that was when I still had the boys to help carry me through. Now, though, they're gone. They're about to be living out their dreams. I always knew they'd get discovered and leave this one-horse town. I just never stopped to think about how much it would hurt me when they did.

Raif

Allowing myself to be herded into Bran's waiting truck when I know Chloe is crying in my mother's basement is the hardest thing I've ever had to do. I know it's what has to be done, but I still feel like I'm leaving half of myself behind. I don't know that I'll ever forget the sight of her standing there trying to hold herself together so I can do what's best for the band. It's not right that we're going without her.

"Penny for your thoughts," Luke murmurs from beside me in the backseat.

I swallow around the lump in my throat and use my sleeve to wipe the tears from my face. "Just don't like leaving her behind."

Luke nods. "I don't either," he admits. "She's one of us, but we'd have to convince her of that." He sighs. "I don't think she feels like she belongs anywhere, honestly. Her mother saw to that." He sounds angry again and I tamp down the jealousy that tends to rise whenever he acts possessive or protective over Chloe. Which is insane because I know he'd never act on it, and I know Chloe doesn't want him that way. Or I don't think she does. I shake myself, focusing on Luke's words and not my raging insecurity.

"She belongs."

"I didn't say *I* didn't know that, Raif, I said she doesn't think it." His voice has more of a bite to it now, and I clench my jaw in response.

"Well I didn't realize that."

"I know, jackass. That's why I'm tellin' you."

Bran clears his throat from the driver seat. "Okay, you two. Cut the shit right now, we have a long drive and then a flight and then we're gonna be spending a lot of time together. So, get over your shit. Now, please."

I wish I could get angry at the intrusion, but we are arguing in the back of his car. And it's become clear to anyone who knows Luke at all how he feels about my girl. And he's right. Now isn't the time for pettiness between us. We're better than this.

Troy surprises me with a calm, "Seconded. You two are driving me nuts." He heaves a sigh. "Look, we all love Chloe in a way, okay. We all want the best for her. Luke, it's not fair of you to make Raif feel bad because he's a dumbass about his lady. You had her first. And he's been distracted over the last decade with the wicked witch bitch who left him at the altar."

Bran murmurs, "Hallelujah." at that. And I blink. I never thought about him having had her first. I knew they'd had sex in high school, because friends talk. And with Troy as a friend of yours, your sexual exploits (or lack thereof) were always up for debate.

Troy continues as though Bran never spoke. Luke looks to be

chewing on his tongue. "Don't get pissed at me, brother. I've known for a long time you were still in love with her. Hence why *I* never made a pass."

Bran sighs when Luke and I both growl. "Not helping." Bran mutters to Troy, "And let's be honest, Chloe'd never go for you."

Troy sounds put out when he says, "You don't know that for sure."

Luke leans forward in his seat, and we say in unison. "Yes, we do."

Troy huffs at us. "Well, fuck you, too. Either way, I'm right. We're about to be holed up together for months away from home. Now is not the time to turn into pussies about this shit. So stuff it back down or whatever you gotta do." He shrugs as if he has no idea how this feels, and to be honest, he probably doesn't. Troy doesn't do connections, doesn't get close. "I think you should write it in a song and let it go. Both of you."

Bran is shaking his head as he drives. "You're an eloquent motherfucker, you know that. We're gonna put you on Dr. Phil as a guest host or some shit."

Luke sighs next to me. "I have no issues with anyone."

I cast him a sidelong glance and clear my throat. "This is new for me. I get jealous, can't help it." I look at Luke again, and ask him something that's been haunting me since Chloe and I got together. "You think I'm bad for her?"

Luke's shoulders sag. "I wish I could say yes and tell you to leave her be." He sounds haggard again. "But, I'm no liar. You just need to pay attention better. You make her happy most of the time."

Relief floods through me at his words. "I'll do better."

Luke nods, his eyes on the scenery flying by us outside his window. "Good."

Troy sits back in his seat and folds his arms over his chest. "See.

This is better than you two being all butt hurt over shit and glaring at each other all the damn time."

Bran shakes his head. "Sure, cuz that was my concern."

Troy shrugs. "Whatever, they're not biting each other's heads off anymore, are they?"

"Just hush, Mother Teresa." Bran turns the radio on and we all shut our mouths and listen to the local country station until it's nothing but static on the speakers.

Nashville is beautiful. Hot and sultry. Good food and amazing music can be found every night downtown. I don't think Troy is ever going to go back home when this is all over. He seems to have found his utopia. Any girl with a twang to her voice seems to set his dick twitching. He'll have bedded every available woman over the age of 17 before we're done recording this album. Typical Troy. Bran, as always, is hyper focused on work. We're in the studio every day, and that's where one hundred percent of his attention is. I don't think he's even realized there are women around us.

Luke hates the heat almost as much as Chloe does, so this climate is a new level of hell for him. He's back in surly Luke mode. He's got a perpetual sneer on his face and at least three times a day, I hear him mutter, "I cannot wait to go home." Tennessee in late September feels a bit like New York in July only on steroids. Some of us are adjusting better than others.

The record label put us up in a house to share on the outskirts of Nashville. It's been something of a challenge, learning to cohabitate with three other men who already have their own routines and quirks. But three weeks in, we're getting used to it. Now that Troy has been informed that clothing is not optional in the main rooms of the house, and his dates are not to be left unsupervised. We woke up one morning to find a chipper little blonde trying to remove the stereo equipment. No one was amused.

Most of our time has been spent working, but at night, we make our way into the city proper to explore. After all, we are tourists when everything is said and done. All four of us have been wanting to see Nashville since we were kids. This is part of the dream for us, too. I wish I could enjoy it more. I am trying to experience everything, trying to take it all in to relay back to Chloe. I'm not having much fun, though.

It doesn't feel right to be enjoying things. Not when missing Chloe is like a constant ache in my stomach, an unreachable itch under my skin. She's meant to be here, too. It pounds through my blood every moment of every day. And I can't keep reiterating to her how much I wish she was here because then I feel guilty.

The boys and I went to the Grand Ole Opry last night and all I could think all night long was how much she would've loved the history of the place, the acoustics and the ambience. She would have been in love with the whole scene. I took pictures and tried to recount every detail when we talked on the phone this morning, but I don't know if I did it justice.

It's been three weeks, but it feels like years since I held Chloe in my arms. We video chat, text and talk whenever possible. I can't tell if it helps or if it just makes me miss her more. She looks tired, not that I'd ever tell her that. And sad. And the sadness is what kills me whenever we talk. The sunshine seems to have fled from her and it hasn't returned. I know it's my fault, and I hate myself for it.

I want her here with me, where she belongs. But I can't ask her to pick between her family's business and me. It wouldn't be fair. I know she takes running the Saloon seriously. Merle wanted her to take over and that's all that matters to her. She won't walk away from that responsibility. Anyway, wouldn't she have said she wanted to come with me when we talked about my move here if that's what she wanted? She's never once said she wants to be here, living with me. She mentioned wanting to see the Opry someday, but that's a different thing altogether.

On a positive note, Chloe has songwriter credit on almost every song we're recording, and that means she'll be getting paid. I don't think she realizes that. I'm gonna keep it as a surprise for as long as possible. The only song she didn't help write was one that Luke and I wrote together since we got here. We took Troy's advice and tried to hammer out some of our feelings for her by writing music together. It's called *Renegade Heart*. It's another surprise. Just something to show her we know we wouldn't be here if it wasn't for her and everything she does for us. She's really the heart of the Renegades, even if she doesn't perform with us normally. She's here with us in spirit, always.

Raif

Six Months Later....

Dell's husband, Rhett, works at a Nashville radio station and he got *Renegade Heart* on the air. People took a liking to it, started requesting it all the time. It hadn't even officially dropped, and we got a call from another Music City artist wanting us to open the rest of their Midwest tour dates. We'd just wrapped filming on our first music video, for *Renegade Heart*. It was beyond surreal. Things just started happening rapid fire.

I had to cancel my planned three-day weekend in White Oak with Chloe, so we could leave to meet the tour in Missouri. She was understanding, but I could hear in her voice on the phone that all was not well. Unfortunately, it wasn't something I could fix now. I left, and life became a whirlwind of travel and performing. It's all exciting, but also exhausting.

Troy is in his element, he was born for this life, I think. Luke and Bran are getting by okay, I think. Tired, but enjoying themselves. I fought against it at first, knowing I'd hurt Chloe more by canceling our visit to tour, but within a week of touring, I was happy with how things were going. I still miss my girl, I want her with me. It's not keeping me from enjoying this experience anymore, though.

I've tried several times to arrange for Chloe to come meet us at a show. I offered to buy her plane ticket, but she keeps saying no. I stopped trying so hard. I don't know if she's just waiting until I return to White Oak to end things or what. It hurts too much to think about it, so I don't. I'm living in the moment.

This is a stadium tour, and it's nothing like the piddling little venues we were playing before. I know we couldn't draw a crowd like we're playing for every night on our own. Not yet, but it's coming. I know it is. I can feel it in my bones. I am lonely but I'm also writing every day, it's fueling my creativity.

Tonight, we're playing to a sold-out crowd in Columbus, Ohio. We are scheduled to do a radio interview in the morning, our first one ever. And then we'll pack it up and get on the bus to travel to the next stop. All in all, life is good.

Currently, I'm waiting for Chloe to video call me, so we can chat on Skype. She missed our call yesterday. She's been missing a lot of our calls lately. I know she's busy, so I try not to let it get to me, but I'm busy, too. I still manage to carve out the time for our calls every day. I don't understand why she can't find a way to do that, too.

Finally, the ring comes that I've been waiting for and Chloe's face is on my laptop screen. My heart sinks at the sight of her. She looks tired. Her big green eyes are bloodshot, dark circles prominent under them. Her pretty hair is up in a messy knot on the top of her head, her small form swallowed up in a hunter green cable knit sweater. She grins at me, a very toned-down version of her normal smile, no sparkle present in her eyes at all. "Hiya, cupcake. Sorry I'm late."

I shrug, smile at her. "It's okay, darlin'," I lie, unwilling to delve into the unpleasant feelings squirming around inside me. "How are you doing?"

She watches my eyes and I see the hint of a smile she'd been sporting disappear. "I'm fine. How's life on the road?"

Fine. *Super*. Now she's even more upset. I swallow down a sigh. "It's okay," I say, not lying. "We've got the hang of it now, I think." This has been happening more and more often lately, too. There seems to be this ever-thickening wall between us that has nothing to do with distance and everything to do with whatever words we're each burying. I don't know how to fix it, how to fix us. I don't know if we'll ever reclaim the formerly easygoing relationship we shared.

I hear voices from her end of the call, and Chloe turns to the door of her office as Zora pokes her head in. "Sorry to interrupt, Chlo, but your mom is out here again." Chloe's shoulders slump and I hear something thump from her end.

"Of course she is," Chloe says, sounding more defeated than I've ever heard her. She looks up at Zora, "I'll be right out." Zora nods, looking sympathetic and then ducks back out again. Chloe turns her attention back to me. "I'm sorry, Raif. I have to go deal with this." She's not even looking at me, though, she's looking beyond me.

"It's ok, darlin', I understand. Can I call you tonight?" She's already standing up from behind the desk.

"If you have time, yes. I'll do my best to answer."

"Ok, I love you." I tell her, but I'm talking to an empty screen. She's ended the call to go deal with Lilly May.

I'm still sitting in my silent hotel room a few minutes later when there's a knock on my door. I get up and let Luke in. He looks at my face and mutters, "Fuck." He pushes me into an armchair. "What happened to you?"

I consider staying silent and brushing him off but discard the idea. Luke knows me too well. "Just my call with Chloe got cut short because of her mom, no big deal." I try to lie, to mask the other, darker feelings that I'm starting to drown in.

"You wouldn't be moping in a dark room because of that."

"Shut up."

"You know I'm right. What else is going on?"

I debate holding my tongue, but the need to talk about this with someone wins out. "I don't think she's in it anymore. I miss her, but I don't think she wants to make this work."

Luke's eyes bore into mine, studying me. He's silent for a few minutes before finally he clears his throat. "I don't want to be a dick, I really don't. And I don't know if this is because it's her, but I think you're full of shit." He holds up a hand when I make to get out of the chair. "Sit down and listen, damn it."

"I don't know if I want to hear it."

"Oh, stop being a baby. I've watched you two for years, tiptoeing around your real feelings for each other. Chloe doesn't believe anyone wants her around, ever. Her mother fucked her up pretty good. I thought you knew that about her." He glances up at me.

"I know she can get that way sometimes. But I didn't know she felt that way about me."

Luke sighs. "Well, she does. You get that she's only ever had us and her grandparents to care for her, right? And Pippa used to give her shit if she caught you looking at her too much."

"What?" I gape at him, truly astounded at what he's saying. "I never caught Pippa being a bitch to Chloe."

Luke shakes his head at me. "Well, you're the only one who didn't. I mean, hello, Chloe spent most nights in your bed and Pippa is definitely the jealous type." He waves me off when I make to interrupt him. "The bigger issue right now, though, is you don't think you're good enough for her. And you both take silence as a personal insult. But you won't talk about shit. So there's no growth and nothing gets solved." I can hear the impatience in his voice and I'm sure this is the absolute last thing he wants to be doing right now.

"I didn't realize you knew all that." I murmur to him.

Luke opens his mouth to retort, but there's a knock on the door and Troy calls out, "C'mon boys! We're gonna be late if we don't leave now."

I sigh as Luke calls back, "We'll be right out." He turns his attention back to me. "Things might be easier to work out if you two were face to face, Raif. We have a break coming up, try and hang in there until then."

Later that night we're leaving the arena, following security to our waiting car, the throng of loud female fans calling our names, asking for autographs and photos. To keep Troy from spawning endlessly across the Midwest, we've put a no fraternizing with fans rule into effect. He hates it, but the rest of us use it as an excuse to look straight ahead and move from one point to the other.

"Raif!" I hear and freeze in place. I know that voice. I turn my head and see the familiar long red hair and blue eyes of my ex-fiancé.

She catches me looking at her and a huge smile splits her face. "Tell them it's okay," she bellows at me.

I shake my head wordlessly and feel someone take hold of my elbow, towing me towards the car. Turning my head towards whoever has hold of me, I see it's Luke looking grim. He glares at Pippa. "No." he says loud enough for her to hear. "Get lost, Satan."

Her overly made up eyes narrow unhappily as she pouts. "That's rude."

Luke smiles at her like a shark. "I don't care if it's rude. The days of me being polite to you are long over." He turns to the nearest security guard and points her out. "Take her picture, please. She's a stalker. We do not want her anywhere near us. Understand?"

The guard looks mildly alarmed and nods, snapping a photo of Pippa and then stepping forward to block her view of us. I turn to Luke, shocked. The guard says, "Ma'am, I'm gonna need you to move along. You don't belong back here."

"Classy, Luke." Pippa snaps at him and steps away from the line, raising her hands in a surrendering gesture.

"Stay away from all of us," Luke says to her, almost genially. "You are *done* causing damage here."

He nudges me on to the car and I climb inside, not looking back. Once Luke follows me in, he points a stern finger at me and says, "Don't even fucking think about it or I'll nut punch you. Understand?"

There's no disguising the anger in his voice. I feel my own temper rise in response. "How stupid do you think I am?"

Troy groans unhappily, looking between us. "What the fuck happened now?"

Luke snaps, "Fucking Pippa is here."

Bran sighs. "Well, he's with Chloe now so she'll have to just go away." His voice is calm, not concerned by the news.

Luke glares at him, too. "When has he ever walked away from Pippa before?" he asks as though I'm not sitting right here staring at him in shocked silence. "And when was the last time he saw Chloe?" He laughs darkly, "It's been almost eight months and he's lonely and they're not connecting and now here comes Pippa." He sounds disgusted with all of us and my fists clench in my lap. "If we hadn't been there, he'd already be back under her thumb!"

Troy mutters, "Fuck me."

I clench my jaw, trying to control my temper, trying to hold back from screaming at my best friend. "Luke." I expel a long breath, trying to bring in positive light and all that crap. "Fuck you, man. I wouldn't ever hurt Chloe that way." My voice shakes from the anger I'm trying to tamp down, the hurt that is invading my chest at learning this is how little he thinks of me. Am I really this giant a fuck up in his eyes? Who else feels this way? Is this why Chloe is pulling away from me now?

Luke shakes his head. "Sure, you wouldn't. Think back on that conversation we had earlier and ask me again why I'm not convinced."

Troy speaks up from his spot next to our driver. "Okay. Enough. Fucking shut up both of you. I'm so sick of listening to you two bitch at each other!"

"Troy, you are not good at this, okay. Stop trying to help." Bran says.

"Fuck that noise." Troy counters. "You two aren't allowed to talk about Chloe anymore. All you do is fight when you do."

"Troy—" I start, but he cuts me off.

"No, I mean it. This is bullshit. Both of you assholes shut up. You need a time out."

Anger boils over inside me but I shut it down, keeping my mouth closed and turning to look out the window. I watch the scenery fly by as we head back to our hotel for the night, trying to hold back everything I'm feeling right now. I might be surrounded by my best friends, but I've never felt more alone. Right now, I'd give anything to be anywhere else with anyone else. I don't want to feel like this anymore, I can't stand it. I can't keep going this way.

20

Chloe

I SLEPT POORLY LAST NIGHT. I COMPLETELY GAVE UP AT FIVE, deciding to start my day with a brisk jog through the early morning quiet of town. My hope was that it would wake me up and clear my head. The opposite happened instead. I spent the entirety of my run obsessing over my increasingly short calls with Raif, the drooping sales at the Saloon. The worsening issues with my mother. I returned home with a heavier heart than when I left.

Most days I wake up feeling lonely, missing Raif. Mornings before were for slow, sweet kisses and runs through town where we pushed each other to keep going. Even before we became a couple, we would share breakfast on my back porch. Look out over the town square as we talked about anything and everything. It was usually the best part of my day. And more than I miss my boyfriend, I miss *those* times. I miss my best friend. I don't think I have ever felt this alone before in my life.

I feel like the longer he's gone, the slimmer the chance is that he's coming back to me when the tour's over. After all, Renegades are becoming famous now. Their single, *Renegade Heart,* is a radio hit. I know for a fact, Troy and Luke both plan on moving to Nashville permanently. Bran has been considering splitting his time between White Oak and Tennessee. No one knows if Raif has made any decisions regarding where he'll make his home when this tour is done. I'm too afraid to ask.

Raif wasn't even the one to share any of that news with me. I heard it secondhand at the Saloon after Luke called his sisters a few weeks ago. I'd like to think that Raif would talk to me before figuring all that out. But I don't know anymore. Our calls have become almost painful. I feel like an obligation that he feels he has to honor. Something to check off his to do list. An annoyance that stands in the way of him really enjoying this experience.

On top of my relationship crumbling, my mother has become impossible to handle. She's now ducking into the Saloon at least twice a week, sometimes even daily. Out of good ideas about how to keep her away, I've begun calling the sheriff every single time she appears. I'm hoping that if she gets arrested for trespassing enough times, maybe they'll actually hold her. Maybe, eventually she'll be wholly discouraged from returning. I don't believe I am that lucky, though.

At only eleven am, I can already feel my control over my emotions slipping. Since my run, my morning's been spent hiding in the office at the Saloon going over the books. This was a mistake. I skipped breakfast, I have no appetite to speak of these days. My stomach is empty, my whole-body throbbing with its hollowness. Desperation has married the grief eating me up inside and now they both color everything. Things are only getting worse as the days go by.

I wish my mother was my only worry. I wish I had a mother who baked cookies and nurtured me. Rather than a mother who slept around, spending her days drunk or high on whatever substance she can find to escape the darkness that's ruined her from the inside. I cut that thought off before it can really take root. I know better than to go down that road. This is the hand I was dealt. I know better than to hope for more. Maybe that's where I went wrong with Raif?

Honestly, I really wish I was with the boys on the road. I'd rather be wrapped up in the chaos of the tour, with my friends, and my boyfriend. Anything would be better than being here pinching pennies and watching my grandfather's dreams die. Without the band in town to perform twice a month, revenue is down at the Saloon. I'm considering closing on Sundays from now on to help us save money. We can't afford to pay our staff for the hours we're currently working. I haven't taken a full paycheck in over a month. Lacey's already quit because I had to cut her hours. She was sweet about it, but I still feel awful. Like I'm running my grandfather's business into the ground.

Between learning to navigate a long-distance relationship with a burgeoning country music star and trying to save my family's fading business, I don't have a lot of time for dealing with my mother's antics. That doesn't stop her from making life more difficult, though. And on top of everything else, today is the one-year anniversary of my grandfather's passing. It took me by surprise, I was paying bills and making notes and then the date clicked in my head and my heart broke all over again.

Not a day goes by that I don't think of my grandfather and wish he was still around. To talk to, for companionship, to take back the responsibility of running his business. I hate feeling like I am failing him. I'm destroying what he and my grandmother built together. I don't know how I managed it, but I did. The truth is right there in front of me in the spreadsheet I've been staring at for the last forty-five minutes.

I keep trying to push through the grief that's been threatening to swallow me lately. I'm failing at that, too, though. My grandfather ran this business all his adult life. When he was alive, it thrived. I don't know if it's because Lilly May has been invading in that domain now that he's gone as she never did when he was alive. I only know it's all on me to protect his legacy, and I'm letting him down. No matter what I do, I can only see one small ray of hope. And even if I try it, it might not work.

Massaging my temples, I try to breathe through the panic in my chest. A knock sounds at my door and then Odetta's red head pops in. "You got a minute, honey?"

I gulp down my encroaching tears and nod. "Course. Come on in. What can I do for you?"

She comes around the desk and motions for me to stand up, and I, as usual, do as she says. Before I can even ask her what's going on, she pulls me into her arms and hugs me tight. The tears burn hotter, making it hard to breathe as Odetta rubs my back and holds me close. After a long moment, she pulls back and brushes my hair away from my face, studying my eyes intently.

"How are you doing?" Odetta asks me, her eyes kind.

I laugh without humor, feeling the tears bubble up inside me once more. "Oh, I'm just peachy. How did I get here, Odetta? When I took over last year this was a successful business. And now we're just hemorrhaging money."

She pats my cheek and moves her hands to my shoulders. "Baby, you are not to blame for that. The business has been slowing down for a couple years now. Merle just never told you. And besides, you never asked for this. You're doing the best you can."

"I never dreamed he'd want me to have this place." I murmur, trying to defend myself even though she just said it's not my fault. I can't help but disagree. He trusted me and I'm wrecking everything he built.

"You were everything to him, honey. I think mostly he wanted to make sure you'd have a way to support yourself no matter what. He didn't want you to have to answer to anyone else because *he* hated that."

I nod, my throat closing on me in my attempt to keep the tears at bay. She seems to understand, though. She pats my cheek again, sighing at whatever she sees in my face. I swallow down the tears and try to smile. "We're gonna have to close on Sundays from now on." My voice wobbles and I square my shoulders, trying to bolster myself.

"That's okay, Chloe. Have you thought about what your next plan of action will be if that doesn't help?" Her voice is soft, uncharacteristically sweet and I know I'm in trouble, because I've earned her pity.

I shake my head. "I mean, we can eliminate lunch next I suppose. That doesn't bring in much revenue and even if you and I are the only ones on the payroll for that time span most days, it's a cut we can make."

She nods at me. "That's definitely something we can do." She seems to weigh her next words for a long moment before speaking. Finally, she licks her lips and asks, "Can I ask you something, honey?"

"Of course."

"Do you even want to run this place?" She practically whispers to me. "It seems to be dragging you down and stressing you out. Especially since the boys left."

I swallow down a hysterical laugh. "I don't know," I tell her. But I think she knows it's a lie. She frowns at me thoughtfully.

"I think you need a vacation. Why don't you go meet up with the boys out west? I think it would do you good. And I can run things here if you like...or we can close up for a week. No one will die if you take a break, honey."

This time I can't hold back the quiet snort of derisive laughter. "I'm not gonna crash his party." I say softly, and I watch her thin mouth go even thinner.

"What do you mean? Did something happen?"

I shake my head, holding up my hand to ward off further questions that I cannot handle right now. "No, no. I'm just..." I sigh, rubbing at the pounding pressure in my temples. "He hasn't said he wants me there," I admit finally.

She hugs me again, which is how I know I must look and sound absolutely pathetic. After a few sniffles from me, she pushes me back gently. "Now you listen here. I've known you and Raif since you were in diapers. That boy loves you, Chloe. He's just an idiot. You need to talk to him, baby. Because he's not gonna read your mind."

I frown at her, going on the defensive. "He's not an idiot, Odetta. Don't talk that way about him, please." I swallow. "It's not his fault if he wants out and doesn't know how to tell me."

She pats my cheek again, smiling sweetly at me despite my rebuke. "Sorry, sweet tart. I call it like I see it." She sighs, studying my face. "You two will find your way out of this." She shrugs. "Or you won't. Either way, I promise you it won't be the end of the world. You'll survive whatever comes."

I'm both bolstered and frightened by her words. I grab her this time, hugging her tight. "Thank you," I say, finally letting the tears slip past my defenses. "I don't know what I'd do without you, Odetta."

She strokes her hand over my hair and squeezes me. "Sweetheart, you have got to learn how to ask for help when you need it. There are so many people who love you and would help you in a heartbeat. You just have to let them."

I turn my face into her neck and allow myself to cry for a moment, enjoying the feeling of someone older, wiser—someone like a parent, hugging me. Someone caring. I can't speak. She allows it for a minute or two and then gently pushes me back again, cupping my face in her wrinkled hands.

"I know you feel adrift without your boys, honey, but you're not alone."

I flinch at her words. They're not my boys. Not anymore. They left me behind when they hired a new manager without even warning me. I never technically had the job, but I certainly did it. And I never realized how much it meant to me to feel like I was a part of them until I didn't have it anymore.

Raif

Two days after Pippa showed up after our show, I'm woken up to the sound of someone pounding on my hotel room door. I groan and hide my head under my pillow, hoping whoever is out there will just go away if I ignore them long enough. We left Columbus right after the radio interview and rode the nine hours to Denver without speaking to each other. It was a long, silent ride. Normally, we all talk and goof around but this time, it was so quiet it actually felt oppressive. I don't know what to say to any of them anymore. I'm tired of learning how low an opinion they all seem to have of me.

I'm so glad this tour is almost over, I need a break. A weekend to just be on my own and figure out how in the world things got so fucked. And then I need to go home and be with Chloe. That is, once I've figured out how to fix what's gone sideways in our relationship. Right. And then I'll cure world hunger.

By the time we got to the hotel and checked in, it was the middle of the night. I crashed hard. I remember stripping down and falling into my bed. I didn't unpack. Didn't shower like I'd been longing to the whole ride here. Now that I think of it, I didn't even call or text Chloe. Fuck me, I suck.

Whoever's at my door keeps on banging. It has to be Luke, wanting to finish hashing things out. I'm in no freaking mood to deal with any of that right now. Honestly, I'm angry at him. Troy's words about Luke knowing Chloe—what she needs, what she feels—better than I do keep ringing in my head. The fact that he's seen her naked, that she was technically his first, makes me crazy if I think about it too hard. That's not helping.

Furious jealousy coats my throat, souring my stomach. "Go the fuck away, Luke. I'm done confiding in you, so you can turn around and make me feel like shit about things." I bellow, without moving off the bed. I glance at the alarm clock on the nightstand and see it's almost ten am. I might be able to catch Chloe before she goes down to the Saloon for the day if I call her right now. I reach for my phone to check for messages and the banging continues as though I never spoke.

"Would you quit your bellyaching and just let me in already?" Fuck. Fuck, fuck, fuck. It's not Luke. "C'mon Raif, I'm not leaving until we talk." It's Pippa. I set my phone back down on the nightstand, debating what I should do.

I could call security and make a fuss and tell them to get her out of here. The fact that she followed us to Denver is sort of creepy, and I'm sorely tempted to embrace the drama. Or I could just open the door and talk to her so maybe she'll stop trailing me like a bad penny. There's no good option.

Talking to her seems like the path of least resistance. I scramble out of bed, fumbling to open my suitcase and pulling out a pair of sweatpants to put on as I stomp towards the door bare-chested. Why the hell can't she just go away? I don't need this hassle right now. Nothing good will come of this. I know that already, in the pit of my stomach. If Luke—or any of the guys—see her, I'm screwed. Luke will most likely punch me. And I'd deserve it. Any of them would tell Chloe and I don't know if our relationship could handle that at the moment.

I pull open the door and see Pippa standing there looking cool and collected now that she's got her way. She's wearing a form-fitting black wrap dress that just hits her knees and leaves way too much of the creamy skin of her chest on display. Her red hair is coiled in perfect curls that fall down her back. Three-inch black heels make her almost as tall as me. She's after something for sure. I straighten and force my eyes away from her body and back to hers.

"What do you want? And how did you find out where we were staying?" I snap at her, trying to ignore the way my body heats just at the sight of her looking like this. She might be gorgeous, but she's nothing but trouble for me.

She steps forward and lets her body brush up against mine as I stand in her way. "Really? It can't be that hard to figure out, Raif. I want you back." She ignores my question about how she knew where we were. Typical Pippa.

She leans up as though she means to kiss me, and I step back fast to keep her from her goal. She takes the opportunity to slip by me, into my room, smiling wide, satisfied with my reaction. I played right into her hands.

My head pounds with rage and exhaustion, all I want is for her to go away, but I know that won't be happening. Not until she has her say. So instead I slam the door shut and turn to her, noting how she flops down on my bed like she belongs there. Like she has the right to just walk back into my life after the way she humiliated me over the summer. In her mind, I guess leaving me at the altar wasn't unforgivable? I don't know, but I do know that Chloe will *never* be okay with this.

"I'm not available." I tell her, leaning back against the closed door. My goal is to keep my distance from her. I don't want to give her any ideas.

She smiles at me like she's already won. She leans back on her elbows, crossing one of her legs over the other, giving me a clear view of the scarlet panties she's wearing. I avert my eyes, keeping them on her face. "You're not available," she repeats. Like it's a joke, something funny I've said to make her laugh. "Everyone's available, baby, don't you know that by now?" She leans back so her cleavage is displayed at the best angle and I cross my arms over my chest, glaring down at her. I'm not going any closer.

"You're wrong, Pip." Shaking my head at her audacity, I think back to all the talk, the way she ran my name through the dirt back home, made a fool out of me. "That explains the rumors that always followed you around, though. You were open for business to anyone who wanted you, weren't you?" At her angry look, I correct myself. "No, I'm sorry, not *anyone*. Just anyone who might get you out of there someday."

She hisses at me like an angry cat but then smooths out her face, making her voice saccharine sweet. "I know I hurt you, Raif, and I'm sorry, but here I am. I want to make things right. What can I do?" She sounds confused as to why I'm not falling back into where we left off. She tilts her head at me, her blue eyes glittering wickedly. "Do you want to punish me?"

I ram my fingers through my hair, tugging on it to try and tamp down the desire to do just that. I don't hit women. Never, for nothing, doesn't matter. I am *not* my father. But this woman brings out the absolute worst in me. And she'd get a kick out of destroying me, she always has.

"You didn't actually. You woke me up. Saved me from making the biggest mistake of my life." I say, enjoying the way her whole body stiffens at my words. "I need you to listen very carefully and hear me Pippa." Her eyes narrow to slits, but I push on. "*I am in love with someone else. I don't want you anywhere near me.*"

She sits up straight up on the bed, tension radiating off her. She hugs herself, looking almost sad for a moment. I can see the anger simmering underneath the façade, though. "Who?" she asks after a few moments. As if she has the right to that information.

"It doesn't matter who, it's not you. I'd like you to leave now."

She pouts at me. "So, I know her then." She studies my face. "From back home?"

"If I tell you who it is, will you just leave?" I ask, desperate to get her out of here before one of the guys comes looking for me.

She purses her painted lips, considering. "Fine. Who is it?"

"It's Chloe."

She throws her head back and laughs like I've just told her the funniest story ever and my jaw clenches tight. I don't know why she thinks this is funny. I don't know what reaction I was expecting, but after the things the guys were saying the other night, I thought her head might explode with anger.

Hands on my hips, I glower at her. "Why is that funny, Pippa?"

She's still laughing, hand on her ribs, as though they're aching from her mirth. "Chloe?" She covers her mouth and lets out a long breath. "Of course it's Chloe." I glare at her until she continues. "She's been in love with you forever. An easy rebound." She shrugs as if Chloe herself is inconsequential.

"She's not a rebound." I bite out through my clenched teeth.

"I've been in love with her forever." I watch the laughter fade from her face and she stands up from the bed.

She comes closer, her red tipped finger wagging at me, "Don't be an asshole."

I grin, enjoying the anger on her face. "Just being honest."

Her face flushes but her voice stays calm. "It can't be serious, or she'd be here. She was always in the middle of all the band's business. If you two were something important, she'd be here. But she's not. I'm not worried." She sounds impressed with her own logic.

"Why she's not here is none of your concern. I answered your question. It's time for you to go now. Don't make me beg." I step away from the door, so she can get out.

She steps closer to me, close enough that when she reaches out her hand, her red finger nails scratch lightly across my naked chest. I can't hide the shudder that runs through my body at the touch. Pippa's shark smile blossoms on her pretty face, homing in on my weakness. "C'mon Raif," she cajoles, pressing closer to me so I can feel the heat of her body. "You've been on tour for how long now? Going without...." She lets her words trail off as her fingernails graze back up from my stomach to my ribs, her meaning clear.

My mind blanks of all thought and my whole body aches with desire that's been unsated for far longer than I've gone since I was a teenager. I swallow hard and look down at her, surprised to see she's right in front of me now, no space between our bodies. I don't know how that happened. While I'm trying to figure it out, she leans in closer, until her mouth is mere inches from mine.

Fuck me.

Chloe

I'VE WORKED OUT A NEW PLAN FOR THE SALOON. I'M
cautiously optimistic about it. Odetta, Zora and I pow-wowed for
hours in my apartment one night after closing. Zora seconded Odetta's desire to help any way she can. In the midst of all this mess, I'd
forgotten that they were my friends, too. And just because Merle left
me the business, it doesn't mean I have to do everything on my own.
Having other people to plan with, especially two smart women I
already trust, helped immensely.

Starting tonight, we're holding a weekly karaoke contest. From
our research, it's something that people of all ages seem to enjoy.
And it's not expensive for us to implement. Tonight, is Saturday
night, our busiest night of the week and if this catches on, we'll add a

second night to spread the business over the course of the week. I have a good feeling about it.

If only things had improved in other aspects of my life. I haven't actually spoken to Raif in almost a week. We've texted, which, considering how much he loathes it, is devastating if I let myself obsess over it. He says he hasn't had time to video chat. I don't want to think he's lying to me. I'm trying not to think too much of it. However, there is an itch under my skin, a buzzing that is taking over all my thoughts. It's screaming at me that something isn't right.

My only consolation is that the tour will be over soon. When he comes back home, hopefully things will be decided one way or another. Maybe I should say if he comes back home after the tour, things will be decided. Right now, I can't help feeling like everything is up in the air with us. I feel like he's hiding something from me, that's the only time he ghosts on me. When he feels like he's done something wrong, when he's ashamed of himself. The thought makes my blood go cold.

I'm shaken from my troubling thoughts by a customer saying my name. I grin, handing over their bottle of Blue Moon. Looking around, I feel pride in our plan blossoming in the wake of the hollowness thinking about Raif brings. I called in a favor and the local country station has been promoting the karaoke contest all week for me. As a result, the Saloon is packed tonight. More packed than it's been in ages. I feel hopeful for the first time since Raif left town.

People are waiting four deep at the bar when Lacey comes in with a group of her friends, waving hello and moving towards the stage. That's where Zora is getting the people who came for karaoke situated. I'm surprised to see Lacey, but also glad she came. I was worried she would stay away since she doesn't work here anymore. With any luck, I'll be able to hire her back soon.

It seems like half the town is here tonight, the radio must've really helped spread the word. Or Odetta's friends telling everyone they crossed paths with did the trick. The crowd isn't just full of younger people, there's seniors in here, too. Along with middle aged folks. Hank Warner is twirling Fern Allen around the dance floor like he does this every weekend. He looks to be having the time of his life. I've never seen him dance when he was here before. And he's usually not here at night. This is nuts.

At 8:00 pm sharp, Zora climbs up on the stage. She's dressed in baby pink from head to toe, her dark curls loose around her heart-shaped face, her mocha skin glowing. Wearing jeans and a silky looking top that doesn't want to stay on her left shoulder, converse on her feet, she's absolutely gorgeous.

She taps on the microphone and the bar goes quiet. "Whoa, that's nice," she says, laughing. "I like this. Welcome to the inaugural Saloon Karaoke Contest!" The room explodes with applause and hoots. I grin bigger, feeling like maybe I finally did something right for this place. "If you haven't signed up yet, you have five minutes before we're closing it down for this week, so get in while you can. Otherwise, you'll be at the top of the list for next week." She gestures to the clock. "We'll begin at 8:30 sharp folks, so warm up those vocal chords and get ready!"

She steps down and makes her way to the bar through the throng of people. She comes around the bar and bumps her hip into mine. "This is gonna work, Chloe." She says with a huge smile on her face, and then she begins filling orders to help me clear out the crowd. I smile at her and nod, to show that I heard her. I send up a little prayer to whoever might be listening that she's right.

The bar is still hopping two hours into the karaoke contest. I've got Bobby, one of the bouncers, refilling the beer coolers behind the bar because I can't leave. Odetta has even popped out from the kitchen to help a couple times when things were getting hairy. I haven't been able to look at receipts obviously, but it looks like karaoke is a success. People seem to be having a blast and they're drinking while they do it.

I don't see her when she comes in, I'm too busy mixing a Long Island Ice Tea for Hank. I hear the murmur that goes through the crowd at the bar, though. *Pippa*. Her name is whispered over and over, and I keep my attention on my task. I cannot believe she has the nerve to come here after the way she left things with us.

I look up to give Hank his drink and she's pushed her way to the front of the line at the bar. Typical Pippa. She's dressed simply for her. A Renegades tee shirt that she can order from their website and a pair of blue jeans. Super casual for Pippa, especially on a Saturday night. I don't want to think about what it means that she's wearing a Renegades shirt when she was never supportive of the band before they were discovered.

I ignore her fake, shaky smile and move to the next customer, filling orders until there's a lull in business. I look over and she's made herself comfortable on a stool, staring at me with barely masked annoyance. "What are you doing here?" I ask her, wanting her to go away.

"I deserve that, I guess." She sighs woefully. "I'm sorry about the things I said before, Chloe. I'm home again." She shrugs as though things should be self-explanatory. "I thought we could talk, patch things up. You're my best friend, you know?"

I snort at her. "We were never best friends, Pippa. You tolerated me because I was *Raif's* best friend. You used me to have someone to do your bidding, to make yourself feel better about how shitty a

167

person you are. And I was dumb enough to mistake that for friendship for far too long, but that's done now. How about the truth this time?"

Her face flushes but she just frowns. "I'm sorry you feel that way." I meet her eyes and she continues. "I'm here because Raif and I have worked things out. And you're still his best friend, I'm assuming? We're gonna have to find a way to be around each other."

My entire body goes cold at her words, but I force a derisive smile. "More lies, Pippa. Raif is with me now. Which you obviously know. That's why you're here." I try to hide the trembling in my hands at the unwanted suspicions that are now zinging through my mind. He wouldn't do that to me. He wouldn't do that to anybody.

She laughs at me. "Maybe he rebounded with you when I was gone, Chloe. I can promise you I saw him three days ago and he still wants me." I look at her full in the face then and see no trace of deception anywhere, no tension, no anger. Just triumph.

I fist my hands in the rag I was about to use to wipe the bar down with and force a breath out through my mouth. "I'm no rebound." I bite out, trying not to think about the fact that I haven't actually talked to Raif in days and this would be a really good reason as to why. "He loves me." I say, feeling pathetic as I am forced to try and convince her of something I still don't understand.

She laughs again. "Both of those can be true, you know. Maybe he does, I don't know. I don't care. I had him for years, it won't take me long to whip him back into shape."

My anger spurts hot and I bang my fists on the bar. She still thinks of him as nothing but a possession. Someone she can twist around her finger and destroy. Even if I wasn't with him, I wouldn't be okay with that. Not anymore. "You think it's that easy? He's a person, Pippa! And you never deserved him, you never knew him.

You're not going to get me thinking he betrayed me. I know him. I trust him. Get the fuck out of here now."

She doesn't even sound concerned. "But you let him go off on his own. How long has it been? Six months? You think a man's gonna go without for that long and then turn me down? If you do, you're a bigger fool than I thought."

We've gathered a crowd of curious onlookers now, and I force my body to straighten up and hold the traitorous tears at bay. I can't do this here. I don't want to be the talk of the town. I don't want to ruin the progress we've made with the business tonight.

My voice wobbles when I speak, but I can't help it. "I think you're a whore, and you're not welcome here. Get out of my bar. Now."

She laughs again. "Oh, you're going to kick me out now? Can you really afford to do that, Chloe? Don't you need every dime to keep the place going? Isn't that why you didn't go with Raif when he left town?"

"That's none of your business. Get out." I'm gripping the top of the bar tight, trying to keep myself from launching over it. Right now, I'm dying to pull her hair out at the roots.

She stays where she is, perched on the barstool, mocking me with her very presence. "I'll leave but it won't change anything. I stole my man back from you. Oh, he made noises about loving you, about how he wanted me to go. But I still had him inside me three days ago. He couldn't say no when I showed up at his hotel room door and did all his favorite things." She looks disgusted at me for a moment. "How could you think he'd want you if he could have me back?"

My heart shatters and the bottom drops out of my stomach at hearing her say it so plainly. I know my face is showing the devastation inside me, but I can't do anything, I can't even speak right now.

This hurts, and the truth is there in her words, what I've always worried about. This is worse than anything I've ever felt. She's right. I'm a fool.

Before I can figure out what to even say to her, Pippa lets out a whimper and I see Odetta behind her, with a fist full of Pippa's red locks. Apparently, she's heard enough. With the hair fisted at the nape of her neck, Odetta yanks Pippa off the barstool. "That'll be enough out of you. Get the hell out and don't come back. I don't care how many blowjobs you gave the deputy, I'll have you thrown in a cell if you ever come back in here."

Odetta drags an enraged and screaming Pippa to the door.

"Let me go, you old bitch!"

Odetta ignores her and motions to Frankie, the bouncer at the door. He opens the door for her and Odetta pushes Pippa outside. She shakes her hands out, as though getting rid of something vile that touched her skin.

Frankie closes the door in Pippa's face as she makes to come back inside. Odetta says, "You ever let her in here again and your ass is fired. You hear?" He nods vehemently, not even looking to me for validation of the statement.

I'm still standing there like a statue, my brain as empty as my chest feels right now as Odetta comes back around the bar. I shake my head, feeling dazed; empty. Stupid. I'm so stupid. Odetta nudges me back a little. "Honey, go splash some water on your face and get back out here, okay? Don't you let her in your head. You wait until you can talk to Raif."

I nod, still voiceless, and escape into the office to do as she said.

After all, what else can I do? It's not like I can call Raif right now and demand answers. He's on stage performing right now, in some city I'll never see across the country. I have to be strong, get through the night. Later, when I'm not feeling so raw, hopefully, I'll call him and tell him he has to have the time to talk to me tonight or we're done.

I tamp down the urge to just lock the door and sob. I have to go out and pretend I wasn't affected by that whole scene now. I don't know that I'm that great an actress. But I have to try.

23

Raif

THE SHOW IN PORTLAND WAS AMAZING. THE CROWD WAS INTO it, our merchandise is selling and there's actually enough time tomorrow to do some sightseeing before we hit the road. All in all, it was a good day. I should be flying, all four of us should be. But I'm clutching my cell phone to my ear, Chloe's voice wobbling on my voicemail. "Raif, you need to call me as soon as you get this."

I see Luke's head tilt to the side, his jaw rigid. Clearly, he heard the message. Super. He's not speaking to me at the moment. None of them are actually. The tables turned quickly when Luke, of all people, saw Pippa leaving my hotel room. I was half naked, and so even though I had her by the elbow, literally dragging her from my room, he jumped to conclusions. He told Bran and Troy what he saw when they heard us yelling at each other in the hallway.

Other guests at the hotel had come out to see what was going on. I'm sure our record label will be thrilled if they find out about us causing a public scene. Things are frosty now. The only time we act like we want to be near each other is when we're on stage. We have four shows left on this tour and we can do what we want for a month. We have to be back in Nashville for the promotion of our debut album the month after that. The break can't come fast enough at this point. Right now, it feels like getting signed was the worst thing that ever happened to me.

"Is she okay?" Luke asks, his voice attempting civility.

I turn my head to look at him full on, surprised he's speaking to me. I know it's only because he's worried for Chloe, but I'll take it. I'm in a mess and I know it. "I don't know, doesn't sound it."

"You gonna call her back? Or you gonna keep on being a pussy?" He asks me, his voice biting.

"I'll call her back as soon as we get back to the hotel." I snap back at him. "I'd rather at least have the illusion of privacy."

He sighs. "Sorry, just you're fucking this all up, Raif. I can't sugarcoat it."

"You think I don't fucking know that?" I bark at him. "I have to tell her everything, and even though nothing happened, she's gonna think the worst just like you assholes all did. I'd wait and just tell her when I see her, but she'll see right through it. Video chat with her, she's gonna take one look at my face and see that something's gone on. Same with the telephone, she'll hear it in my voice."

"You think she doesn't know something's up right now?" Luke asks angrily. "If you believe that, you're an idiot."

"I don't know what to do, Luke! I don't want this to hurt her and I know it's going to. No matter what I do, I'm here and she's there and shit's just unraveling."

Luke opens and closes his mouth without speaking.

Bran speaks up startling me. I'd forgotten he and Troy were even in the car. "And where's Pippa?"

I think about Chloe's voice on the message. Then I recall Pippa's rage when we had her evicted from the hotel after she showed up at my door. "*Fuck me,*" I groan.

When I get into my hotel room, I close my door and pull out my phone again. I've been putting this off for far too long already and I know that. I've probably made everything much worse. Chloe answers on the first ring, her voice is sad. "Raif?"

I can hear the sounds of people talking, the clink of bottles and glasses, laughter. Thomas Rhett on the jukebox. A wave of homesickness hits me hard and I have to fight back tears. I miss her so much, miss home. I miss sitting at the bar, watching her work her magic, charming people left and right without even trying. Miss waking up to her every morning, holding her in my arms as I fall asleep at night.

I hear a soft click and the other sounds cut off and I know she must have ducked into the office, so we can talk privately. I steady my voice. "Hey, darlin', I'm really sorry we haven't spoken in so long. It's good to hear your voice." I swallow and ask, "Are you okay?"

A lifetime seems to pass in silence before I hear her shaky breath skitter over the line. "I don't know." Then before I can say anything else, she continues. "Pippa was here earlier."

She pauses, and I interject, "I can explain, Chloe, I swear."

I hear her breath catch, hear the tears in her voice now. "So, it's true." She sounds defeated, and all I want in the world right now is to hold her.

"She tracked me down in Columbus, trailed us." I can hear her

174

crying, even though I know she's trying to hide it. "Chloe, don't cry, please. I swear to you nothing happened."

She sounds choked when she speaks next. "If nothing happened, what is there to explain?" She sniffs and seems to be collecting herself before she continues, her tone more accusatory now. "You swore I wasn't a rebound, Raif. You promised me that this was for real. I trusted you, I believed you and all along, you just wanted her back?"

She doesn't sound angry, per se, more hurt, but her words rankle my already overstretched temper. "How is it my fault that she found me? What else was I supposed to do?"

Her temper fires to life in response, her voice louder now. "I don't know, Raif? Maybe don't fuck her when you're supposedly in love with me?"

I can hear it in her voice that she really believes I did that to her. I can't believe this is happening. She's the one person I always thought would believe me above anyone else. I never thought I'd have to defend myself against untrue allegations with Chloe. I swallow hard around the tears that are prickling against my eyes. Maybe this was all a huge mistake. I knew better than to reach for things I don't deserve.

"You think I'd do that to you." There's no anger in my voice, now. Just acceptance of my reputation among the people I love. "You believed whatever line she fed you. Almost like you've been waiting for this to happen. I can't keep doing this, Chloe. At some point you have to have some faith in me, in *us*. I can't be the only one trying to make this work."

Chloe's voice is small. "I don't know what to believe anymore. You were suddenly too busy to talk. And here she comes, telling me how I was a fool to think you'd want me and oh she had you inside her three days ago. I didn't know what to think."

Anger at Pippa blossoms in my chest, around the hurt that Chloe thinks so little of me. I can hear the sincerity in her words, she doesn't seem to understand how I feel about her. Even though I've told her a thousand times. "Chloe, I love you, I do. I don't want anyone but you, but this right here, this is not my problem. It's yours. We aren't gonna make it if you don't have trust in me."

"I don't know if I can, Raif." Her voice cracks on the words, and I hear a sob from her end of the line. "I love you, I want to be with you, but I don't know if I can keep doing this." I hear her pull in a deep breath. "I think I need some time...."

"Okay," I say softly, as tears drip down my face. "I'm here if you want to talk."

She chokes back a sob. "Okay." She hangs up without saying goodbye. I drop my face in my hands, let the bleakness wrap around me.

Chloe

THE GOOD NEWS IS THAT KARAOKE WAS A HUGE HIT. WE doubled the revenue we've been averaging on Saturdays for the last month or so. I should be happy about that. I should be relieved that Raif didn't cheat on me with Pippa. I can't get there, though. I can't trust love and happiness, and I don't know how to fix that. Also, I've become work for my boyfriend which was the last thing I wanted.

I don't know what to think about any of it. Raif didn't argue with me when I said I needed time. I can't obsess over his motives. I'm so angry that I let Pippa get in my head and make everything worse between him and me. I know better, I know what she's like and I fell for her nonsense. I'm sure she's laughing it up wherever she is now. If she's still in town, she hasn't been stupid enough to test Odetta's patience by coming into the Saloon.

The last two days have passed in a haze. I haven't left the Saloon at all. The nonstop spring rain mirrors my mood, keeping the skies gray and the temperature cool. Three days is too much hiding and I can no longer avoid the world outside of the Saloon. I promised Daisy I'd meet her for lunch at the diner where she works. I leave the Saloon in Zora's capable hands and step outside into the sunshine, breathing deep the fresh air. I don't want to be out and about, I'm sure the town is talking about my exchange with Pippa the other night. But I can't let Daisy down.

I cross the busy town square, taking a shortcut to get to the diner. I walk at a slower-than-normal pace, lost in thoughts of Raif. I can't help but wonder what he's doing right now. If he's missing me as much as I'm missing him. I don't know if that's possible. I miss him so much it's a physical ache inside.

My eyes are on the sidewalk, looking for puddles so I don't wreck my favorite sneakers when I walk right into someone. Feeling like a jerk, I reach out to make sure the other person doesn't fall. "I'm so sorry," I begin by rote, but cut off when I look up and see it's Pippa. "And never mind." I say, sourly, dropping my hands back to my sides.

From the looks of things, she was too busy looking at her cell phone to look at where she was walking. She frowns at me. "Gee, thanks." Her voice is snotty, and rather than engage further with her, I try to detour around her. To move along on my path towards the diner and Daisy.

Pippa has other ideas, though, she turns around and follows me, walking a half step behind me. "Where are you going in such a hurry?"

"None of your business. Leave me alone." I move faster, but her legs are longer than mine. She jogs a bit to get in front of me and then stops, halting my progress again.

"Where are you going? According to the gossips, you've been hiding in the Saloon for the last two days. What could have possibly drawn you out of your hidey hole?" Her voice is pure venom but instead of cringing back from her, like I usually do, I step forward and meet her challenge.

I'm so tired of everything about this woman. I am done being the bigger person. I'm done worrying about what the town will say, what people will think. Fuck them all, I'm going to say my peace this time. For myself, and for Raif. He's mine, damn it. And I'm his. I need to make sure she can never come between us again.

I move closer until I could reach out and snatch her long hair if I wanted to, she left it down today, it'd be easy. She'd never expect it from me. Instead I plant my hands on my hips, let my own voice ring out, let my anger show. "I'm going to have lunch with Daisy, not that it's any of your damn business. Nothing in my life—or Raif's—is your business. So back off and leave both of us the hell alone!"

She looks shocked for half a second and then her face transforms with delight. "You—the best friend who used to sleep in his bed—are going to tell *me* to back off! That's rich!" She shakes her head, two livid spots of color high on her cheekbones. "He might have been taken in by your giant, save-me eyes, but I never was. I knew you wanted him, I knew you were using your whore of a mother as an excuse to cozy up to him."

I think about those nights, the fear that was a living thing in my chest, and force myself to laugh in her face. I will not give her the satisfaction of seeing those words affect me. "You don't know him at all. That's the crux of the whole problem, Pippa. You don't give a damn about anyone but yourself and you never have. And for some reason, he's never seen how wonderful he is, so he allowed you to treat him like shit. But he never really let you get to know him and you were okay with that. Until you threw him away one too many times and he decided to move on!"

"And of course, you were right there to help him along with that, weren't you? Just like your mother," she says, trying to play the victim.

I shake my head, keeping my face calm despite the rage her words bring to life inside me. "Nope. You're wrong. I was his friend, Pippa. *He* made the first move," I tell her, relishing the anger on her face. "And the second and the third. He said, 'I love you' first, told me he'd loved me forever," my voice shakes with emotion. "But he didn't think he deserved me. *You* were the punishment he inflicted on himself for all those years!"

Her face goes white with rage and I watch in shock as she opens and then closes her mouth without saying anything. She looks like a fish out of water, her mouth gaping. It looks like she might be breaking down for real this time. The tears that slip out of her eyes are real as she mutters angrily, "You two deserve each other, alright." Then she turns and flees the town square.

When I look around, I see there are several small groups of people gathered around, watching our fight with apt interest. I don't even care what they're saying. I didn't say anything I didn't mean, nothing I'd want to hide. I'm done caring about what everyone else thinks. I walk on to meet Daisy and carry on with my day. Anyone who gives a damn about my argument with Pippa can get a life.

I enter the diner and conversation hushes all around me. "Get a life." I mutter.

Daisy comes bouncing over, her curls semi-tamed into a high ponytail. She grabs me up in a tight hug, "I feel like I haven't seen you in months!" she says.

I grin at her. "I know, I've been too busy working." I hug her back, feeling better about life in general at seeing her. "Is it break time or am I early?"

She smacks a kiss to my cheek. "No, you are exactly on time, like usual. I already put our order in, I hope you don't mind."

I laugh. "What's for lunch?"

"Well, Mom said you were too thin the last time we saw you, so I ordered you the bacon double cheeseburger with the fries and onion rings. And a chocolate shake. And I'm supposed to force you to have some pie for dessert." She says all this very fast, as though if she breathes between words, she won't get the chance to finish.

Laughing, I hug her again, leading her to an empty booth by the window that looks out over the square. "Well, you might have to roll me out of here when we're done, but that all sounds good to me right now. I haven't eaten yet today."

She giggles, and we settle in at the table to wait for our lunch. And for a little while, I feel like everything might be okay.

I'm dreaming. And I know I'm dreaming because my grandparents are both alive. We're in the Saloon, of course, because that's where they spent most of their time when they were alive. And I'm so happy to be on the customer side of the bar, rather than behind it mixing drinks and serving people. I miss this view of the Saloon, when I could just sit back and watch the mini dramas of small town life unfurl in front of me.

I miss watching my grandparents banter back and forth, the depth of the love they shared apparent in everything they did together. They would sneak me in and let me sit by the jukebox when I wasn't technically supposed to be on the premises. It kept me away from home, away from my mother and whatever she got up to there. They tried their best to protect me from my mother and her lifestyle. My grandfather is still trying to protect me, by leaving me the Saloon. Whether I wanted it or not, he left it in my care.

I'm watching Odetta and Hank Warner dance around the floor together, the Saloon is otherwise empty. My grandparents join them as I watch from my bar stool. The jukebox plays *My Favorite Memory* by Merle Haggard and they twirl around together. I sit, watching them, my heart aching with loneliness. Even in my dreams I can't escape it.

Despite my epiphany with Pippa earlier, I didn't call him. I don't exactly know what to say honestly. I know I'm better for him than anyone else, I know he's the only one I'll ever want. But the trusting that we can work, that's what I struggle with. And I can't keep doing this to him. He deserves me to be all in this with him. No more reservations. Until I know I can do that, I can't call him.

Suddenly, the jukebox stutters to a halt, and a loud grating beep replaces it. The noise is everywhere, and then there's the overpowering stench of smoke. Something isn't right, no something has gone very wrong. I jerk upright on the couch in my apartment above the Saloon, coughing, looking around frantically for the source of the thick black smoke billowing everywhere around me.

Terror seizes my heart and I hear the crackling of flames from somewhere. But where? I can feel the heat, sweat is pouring off my body. I'm still frozen on the couch. I don't know what to do, I've never prepared for this. I tentatively touch my bare foot to the hardwood floor in front of the couch and yank it back again. The wood is blazing hot. I gulp and then choke and cough on the fumes I inhaled.

I grab for my cell phone off the coffee table and attempt to peer through the smoke. Going downstairs is obviously out of the question, but if I can get to the back door and my porch, I can get out that way. I turn the flashlight function on my cell phone on, surely, I can use it to illuminate a safe path out of the apartment.

It's no good, though. I can't see my hand in front of my face in here, even with the flashlight on. The air is thickening by the second, the heat ratcheting higher and higher, and the crackling of the flames I can't see through the smoke is getting louder. I'm convinced the floor is about to be engulfed at any moment. There's no way I'm going to get off of the couch without damaging my feet.

Forcing myself to think of the apartment's layout, I close my eyes for a moment. It's an open floor plan. I recall the coffee table in front of the couch, the entertainment stand beyond that, housing the television and stereo. But the door outside is in the other direction. I need to go behind the couch, which should be open space until I hit the kitchen. From there, I can go on through and out the sliding glass doors, onto the porch.

If I can get outside, I will be safe. That's the only thought in my head as I lift my shirt over my mouth and nose and launch off the couch, crying out at the burning on my bare feet. I dash over the burning floorboards, crashing into walls as I navigate the darkness. I don't take two steps before I'm hacking, my lungs burning with the smoke I'm inhaling, even through my shirt.

Tears sting my eyes, making it even harder to see and I try to stay calm through the panic surging through me. There's a voice in my head echoing that I'm going to die here tonight. Finally, I dance my way on tiptoes all the way across the charring linoleum and make it to the back door. I try to protect my hand from being burned, using my shirt as a barrier between the metal handle of the sliding door and my skin.

It still hurts when I touch the handle, but I think my skin is intact. Small victories, I tell myself and force the door over, so I can stumble out onto my back porch. I fall to my knees on the hardwood, scraping the already sensitive skin of my palms, gulping air into my aching lungs. I cough, my lungs in agony still, the world spinning around me as I try and catch my breath. *Don't pass out now, Chloe, no. You can't. You have to get to the ground and call the fire department. You are not safe yet. Not yet.* The voice is in my head, but it belongs to my grandfather.

I crawl over towards the steps that go down to the ground and see flames leaping, licking their way up, towards me. The fire is eating away at the building inside and out now. A sob escapes my throat. I'm trapped. There's no way down. *No easy way,* I hear Merle say. *Go on, girl, you know what you have to do. Get up.* I look up at the oak tree that grows tall and strong not too far from the building. If I can get to the tree, there's a branch that hangs almost directly overhead on the other side of the deck. I can climb down from there. I can do this.

The roar of the fire is all I can hear, the heat of it chafing my skin, and I stumble back to my feet, crying hard. I don't want to die. The thought of dying without having fixed things with Raif, of never discovering what I want my future to be, it's too much to handle right now. I force it out of my head, think only of putting one foot in front of the other as I practically run on my abused feet to where the branch hangs.

I reach up trying to grab the branch with my fingers, but I'm too short. The flames are almost to the top of the staircase now, coming ever closer. I don't have time to think too much about my next move. I hoist myself up, every motion causing me pain. I try to balance myself on the railing but I'm not steady and before I can even think to reach for the branch, I'm falling.

25

Raif

THE HOSPITAL WHERE CHLOE WAS TAKEN IS JUST AS TINY AS IT was when my mother used to bring me here as a child. The memories of those years of abuse at my father's hands keep flooding my mind, bumping up against the thoughts of Chloe unconscious, hurt and alone. I can't stop trembling and I don't care who sees it. I need to know she's going to be okay. I can't lose her. I can't.

The waiting room is full of people who are here for her. Has been since I arrived. Mom and Daisy are huddled together on one side of me. Daisy is pale, crying into Mom's shoulder as they hold each other. Luke is on my other side, his face tense, his hands fisted in his lap. Troy and Bran are here, too, both silent. Troy's leg is jogging up and down, a nervous habit he's had since we were kids.

Bran doesn't look to be at home mentally. Odetta is pacing the length of the waiting room, wringing her hands. She hasn't stopped moving since we arrived.

Zora and Lacey are present, too; Lacey alternating between tears and making doe eyes at Troy when she thinks no one is looking. Zora's lips haven't stilled in hours, but I never hear her make a sound. I think she's praying. The room is eerily silent, despite the number of people in it. All I can hear is the sound of my heart thundering away inside my chest.

When Mom called me with the news that the Saloon had gone up in flames, and Chloe had been found unconscious and seriously injured, I think my heart stopped beating. I froze up completely. Luke stepped in, leaping into action. He called our promoter and told her we had to cancel the last two tour dates due to a family emergency. She wasn't pleased about it, but he told her we didn't care. He then called Dell, who arranged a private jet to bring us home fast and told us to keep him updated on Chloe's condition.

We've been sitting here waiting for Chloe to get out of surgery for what feels like forever. They said she has first degree burns on her hands and second degree burns on her feet. Multiple broken bones on the left side of her body. Those are the only details we have so far, though. No one knows exactly what transpired. She was found unconscious on the ground underneath the oak tree next to the Saloon.

I don't know what happened, but I can't imagine how scared she must have been there all by herself. I can't think about it. But I can't stop thinking about it either. She shouldn't have been on her own. She should have been with me. That's where she belongs. As soon as she wakes up, I'm never letting her go again. I don't care about the issues we have, about her not trusting things. I can be patient, we'll work it out. She just needs to make it through this.

Hours go by while we wait for news on Chloe's condition. A few doctors come out and spit a lot of medical jargon at us that scares me more than anything else has so far. She survived the surgeries, though. Along with the burns to her hands and feet, she had to have her left leg surgically repaired, it was broken in three places. Her left wrist was also broken, she has a concussion and a gaping wound in her chest that led to a punctured lung. Apparently, she fell from a height and landed on something that impaled her. We were all horrified as we were informed of each new injury she had to endure.

We're told that two of us can go in and see her when she regains consciousness. Odetta has stopped her pacing and now I've started. I can't keep still, knowing Chloe's out of surgery and lying in a bed somewhere all by herself. I want to see her, be able to hold her hand until she wakes up. I need to know she's alive and I won't feel like that's true until I see her with my own eyes.

At some point Bran went out and grabbed coffee and sandwiches for everyone. We're still waiting for word that she's woken up when Sheriff Beale comes into the waiting room. He makes a beeline for Odetta, his face grim. "Any news on Chloe?" he asks her.

Odetta turns to him, her face lost. When she speaks, her voice doesn't have any of her normal sass. "She's out of surgery, we're waiting for her to regain consciousness now, so we can see her."

Mom speaks up from her seat, where she's acting as a pillow for Daisy, who's fast asleep. "What brings you here?"

The sheriff looks around at all of us. "A body was found in the wreckage of the Saloon. Looks to be a female in her late thirties or early forties." He swallows hard, weighing his words before continuing. "Speculation is that it's Lilly May Morris." Odetta visibly flinches and I see Luke go stock still in his chair across the room. "Obviously it'll be a while before we can verify that, but I didn't know if any of you had any idea where she's living these days? A phone number we could try, even?"

Nausea swirls in my gut. I can't imagine how Chloe will take this news if it's true. Mom shocks me by speaking up again. "I saw her the other night sleeping in the gazebo in the square."

Odetta nods at her, "I saw her, too. I have an old phone number, but I don't know if it's any good now."

The sheriff nods. "Okay, well I'll take that. It can't hurt to try it." He looks between Luke and me. "Will one of you let her know that the fire's out? That the fire chief will be in touch when they find what caused it?"

Luke nods as I say, "Of course." An awkward silence falls over the room. Troy sighs loudly.

After a moment the sheriff nods to us. "Okay, then. Thanks, boys."

I nod to him as he ducks back out of the waiting room and leaves. I pick up my pacing again, praying silently to whoever might be listening that Chloe wakes soon.

I'm sitting again when Opal Vereen, one of the nurses on staff, finally appears with good news. She's been working here since she and her son moved to town when I was a kid. Her son Cash enlisted in the service after finishing college, and was deployed. His wife, Johanna, is pregnant and living in my old house now. I can't help but notice that Opal is looking as exhausted as I feel right now. I send a prayer heavenward that Cash is okay.

Mom and Daisy are both asleep, Odetta is sitting sandwiched between Lacey and Zora, the three of them holding each other up. Troy's head is resting against the wall behind his chair, he's fast asleep. Bran has been playing some sort of game on his phone for the last half hour or so in an effort to keep himself awake, I think.

"Are you waiting for word on Chloe Morris?" Opal asks, looking around at all of us camped out in the waiting room.

Luke and I both jump to our feet. "Yes," I say. "Is she awake?"

Opal nods, looking startled. "She is. According to the doctor, two of you can come and see her for a few moments."

Without looking to anyone else, Luke and I both step forward to follow her. She smiles. "Follow me."

Odetta grumbles under her breath before saying, "You kiss her for me and tell her we love her. I suppose I'll have to wait even though I was here first!"

"Thank you, Odetta." Luke says, grinning back at her. She waves us on.

We follow Opal down a maze of hallways until she swipes her id card to let us into the ward. Two doors down on the right-hand side she steps aside and motions for us to go ahead. "When she gets tired, it's time to go, okay?" she says firmly before allowing us to enter. I nod at her and she moves towards the nurse's station in the middle of the floor.

Chloe looks tiny and fragile in the hospital bed, her dark hair like mahogany silk spread out on the pillow behind her head. Her left leg is immobilized, and, in a cast, her left wrist also encased in a cast. Her hands are wrapped in gauze, her feet, too. Her big green eyes are open and alert, though. And hooked on me.

"Raif?" she croaks, looking like the word causes her pain. "Luke!" Tears spring to her eyes and we're both across the room in a heartbeat, hovering uncertainly.

Luke leans down and kisses her forehead. "You should save your voice, sweet tart." His voice is gruff, and I watch as he lovingly smooths her hair away from her forehead and then runs his fingers through the length. "You took a decade off my life, you know?" I can tell he's trying to joke, but he's serious.

Chloe reaches out with her good hand as though to pat him somewhere to comfort him and winces, letting her hand drop back to the bed. "Sorry," she murmurs, her voice raspy from smoke.

"Stop it." He tells her, letting her hair go and folding his hands in front of him, probably to keep from reaching for her again. I can't even be jealous because I understand the desire too well.

She looks to me, almost nervously and I smile down at her, unashamed at the tears in my eyes. I lean down and claim her mouth in a kiss, letting her know everything I'm feeling. She kisses me back fiercely. "Hey, darlin'." I murmur against her lips when I pull back for air.

"What are you guys doing here?" she whispers.

"Hush, love. Luke's right. Save your voice. Nothing could have kept us away when you were hurt."

Luke nods. "Dell Xander sends his regards, too."

Chloe looks shocked that he even remembers her name. "How long can you stay?" she asks.

I grin at her. "I don't know about the other three, but I'm here for the duration, Chloe Jane. I'm your new shadow."

She smiles wide, the sun coming out after the rain and I feel it in my chest. She might be hurt, but she's alive. She's going to heal and be okay. "You're gonna stay?" she looks to Luke and then back to me. "Are you sure that's okay?"

He smiles at her. "We don't have to be in Nashville for another six weeks, sweet tart. I'll be here, too. Things to wrap up before I move for good."

Her face falls a little, but she forces her smile back up. "I'm glad you'll be here for a few weeks, at least. I've missed you guys." She look back at me uncertainly, like she wants to ask me something, but she's afraid to.

I turn to Luke, "Hey, brother, any chance you could give us a moment alone? Maybe go tell the others they'll get a turn eventually?"

I grin at him and he nods. "Of course." He leans down again, places a kiss on Chloe's cheek. "That is from Odetta. She was not happy that I jacked her spot. I expect she'll be in here before long whether the nurses allow it or not."

Chloe smiles happily. "Tell her she's next," she tells him.

Luke salutes her and turns to go, his shoulders slumping. I see the desolation mixed with the relief on his face when he does. I turn back to Chloe, focusing all my attention on her. I kiss her mouth again. "I was so scared," I say against her lips. "I thought I'd lost you. I love you so much."

She loses her smile for a moment. "I thought you did, too." She sounds scared and I wish I could hold her. "All I could think was I hadn't called you. I wanted to. But I was scared, I think."

"It's okay. You're not getting rid of me, Chloe Jane. The hell with everything else, I love you and I want you with me. I should've asked you to come with me before, but I didn't want to ask you to choose between the Saloon and me. It didn't feel right."

Her smile blooms again. "You wanted me to come?"

"Of course I wanted you with me."

"I didn't know." She whispers, tears in her bright green eyes. "I thought you were trying to find a way to ditch me but didn't want to hurt me."

I frown. "Chloe Jane...."

She swallows hard, lets out a painful sounding breath. "I know. I have to trust us, *this*. I'm trying, Raif. I swear I am."

I touch her face, drinking in the sight of her alive and whole for the most part. I know I should ask for details about tonight, I should tell her the sheriff suspects that her mother is dead. But I can't. Not right now. Right now, I'm looking towards the future. "How would you feel about coming to Nashville with me when I have to go back?"

She smiles wide, stealing my breath. "I thought you'd never ask, cupcake."

Epilogue

Raif

Two Months Later ...

CHLOE GOT HER CASTS OFF LAST WEEK AND TODAY WE ARE IN Nashville. We looked online and picked out a house to rent while we're down here. She's been talking nonstop about seeing the Grand Ole Opry so that's where we are today. I'm having a blast watching her take it all in. I've never seen her so excited. I'm loving it.

Things haven't been so easy for her for the last two months. Her business burned to the ground and will cost a pretty penny to rebuild it. She's not certain she wants to right now. But I know she feels like she owes it to Merle to bring it back to life and to its former glory. Also, it turned out that Lilly May was the one who set the fire in the Saloon. It's all purely speculation as to why, but it was a cold night. The sheriff thinks she broke in to get warm. Fire chief says it looked like she built a campfire and probably fell asleep and it caught.

Chloe's looking at all her options, including going to college online. I'm happy for her, I've always thought her not going to college was a waste. As of right now, though, Chloe says she's on vacation, and I'm okay with that. Her mother's death hasn't been easy on her. Even if they weren't close, Chloe's still grieving and I'm trying to be there for her any way I can.

There's a huge crowd here, like usual, and we're still outside, in front of the giant guitars. We've been waiting our turn to take pictures, Chloe not so patiently going up on her tiptoes to see how long the line is ahead of us every few minutes. She's in a blue sundress and converse sneakers. Her long dark hair is pulled back in a messy ponytail and I don't think she's ever looked more adorable. Yet I cringe every time she goes up on her toes, I'm nervous she'll damage her ankle again. This time when she leans up, I tug her into my arms and kiss the top of her head.

"Could you cut that out? You could hurt yourself," I gripe at her.

"Oh cupcake, breathe. I'm not made of porcelain." She giggles.

"Hey, I have reason to worry, Chloe Jane. Half your body was wrapped up in casts just a little over a week ago. I get to be a mother hen without being heckled," I say, true fear reappearing in my chest at the memories. I hold her tighter into my side.

"I don't know about that." She laughs up at me, her face beautiful; open and happy. I lean down and claim her mouth in a kiss. This woman is the center of my universe, the very heart of my being. I would not be me without her and I know that without even a shadow of a doubt.

"I love you, Chloe Jane Morris," I say, and something about my face must tip her off about what I'm going to do because before I've even dropped to my knees in front of her, she has tears in her eyes.

"Raif," she murmurs, her hand fluttering at her chest as I kneel down before her. "What are you doing?"

I smile up at her, chuckle softly and try to ignore the trembling in my hands. I don't think I've ever been this nervous. I reach into my back pocket and pull out a black velvet box. "What's it look like, darlin'?"

She's trembling now, too. And we've garnered the attention of some of the people nearest us. "Are you sure about this?" She looks to be fighting back a smile.

I nod at her. "I've never been surer of anything in my life." I pop open the box, let her see the princess cut diamond with the smaller diamonds and emeralds all around it on the platinum band. She reaches out her trembling hand to me, her eyes like saucers. "Chloe Jane Morris, what do you say? You wanna make an honest man out of me?" She laughs, and I turn serious. "I want you with me for always, Chloe. Will you marry me?"

A few tears slip from her green eyes. "Yes! Yes, I will, of course I will!" She exclaims happily, bouncing up and down, making me nervous again.

I slip the ring on her finger, stand up and swing her up into my arms, spinning her around in a circle, whooping for all I'm worth. "She said yes!"

People all around us are clapping as I set Chloe back on her feet. I stare into her deep green eyes, so happy that I get to call her mine forever now. I take her face in my hands and she meets me halfway for a searing kiss. Everything else fades away as I bask in the feel of her mouth under mine, her hands in my hair, her body pressed against mine. She pulls away and rests her forehead against my collarbone, her hands clutching my shoulders.

I hold her close and marvel at how perfect life can be when you let in the light. And the right people. With Chloe by my side, I know that I can do anything. She's my happy ending, my everything. I can't wait to write the rest of our story, together.

THE END

ACKNOWLEDGMENTS

Tyffani Clark Kemp and Victoria Escobar: you ladies are just everything to me. You are not only my best friends; you're my cheerleaders, my critics, my sounding boards, and I adore and appreciate you both more than you know.

To my husband, **Keith**, who was instrumental in titling this book (and its sequels), I love you. Thank you for supporting me and allowing me to follow my dreams.

Abigail Davies, my design goddess, thank you for your gorgeous brain and your unflagging friendship.

Jaime Radalyac, Shelley Bunnell, Anne Gotham, Amanda Alsterberg, Susan Rodriguez and Rebecca Walters, my lovely beta readers, thank you from the bottom of my heart for taking time away from your families and friends to read Raif and Chloe's story. I love you girls. This book would never have seen the light of day if not for the love and support of my friends and family.

ABOUT THE AUTHOR

Lissa was first inspired to consider a career in writing when she was in high school. Her English teacher recognized Lissa's gift for storytelling and encouraged her love of writing. She has six nieces and nephews whom she adores and a beloved cat who is her baby. Lissa loves the color purple and chai tea and writes poetry under the pen name Bella Sterling.

Under the name Melissa Simmons, she has written one short story with fellow author, Allana Kephart, for the Dare to Shine Charity Anthology. She wrote another short story under the same name for the Best Thing I Never Had Charity Anthology. As Lissa Lynn Thomas, she has short stories in both the This Soldier's Heart Charity Anthology and the Karma Charity Anthology. Lissa's debut solo novel, Renegade Heart, is due out in winter of 2019. Renegade Heart is the first book in the Renegades series.

www.lissalynnthomas.wordpress.com
Reader Group
Newsletter

RENEGADE SOUL

To find out when Luke's book, *Renegade Soul,* will be released, sign up for my newsletter!

Printed in Great Britain
by Amazon